A Witch's Inconvenient Crush

Alexandra Larson

Copyright © 2026 by Alexandra Larson
All rights reserved. Published in the United States of America. No part of this publication may be reproduced or transmitted in any form or by any means, electronic or mechanical, including photocopying, recording, or any information storage or retrieval system, without prior permission in writing from the publishers. No generative artificial intelligence (AI) was used in the writing of this work. The author expressly prohibits any entity from using this publication for purposes of training AI technologies to generate text, including without limitation technologies that are capable of generating works in the same style or genre as this publication. The author reserves all rights to license use of this work for generative AI training and development of machine learning language models.

ISBN: 978-1-970397-00-0 (paperback)
ISBN: 979-8-9874887-8-2 (e-book)

Cover: Author Designed (Photos licensed by author)

First Edition: March 2026

Author Note

This novella is an MM paranormal romance about two seniors in high school (both guys are eighteen years old). There are descriptions of a car crash, discussions of parental death, and sexually explicit content.

You can expect the following tropes: friends-to-lovers, bi awakening, possessive best friend, nerd x jock, secret magic powers, my powers only react this way with you, touch him and you'll be sorry.

Prologue

Twelve Years Ago

Elliot Croft only had one thing he wanted to do during recess. He hated kickball, tag, and had no interest in sitting in the tunnels, gossiping with the girls.

Stone Ridge Elementary's playground had eight swings. Seven, if you considered that the one on the far right made a terrible creaking noise that made Elliot jump out of his skin if he used it.

He would, if he really had to, but it was not preferred. Given there were at least eighty kids on the playground, Elliot had to be at the front of the line when they headed out to recess. To ensure his spot, he would save his dessert from lunch and offer it to the kids in the front of the line to switch spots with him when he wasn't quick enough finishing his spelling work.

His mom understood Elliot's obsession—she was good like that, understanding all of Elliot's eccentricities—and made sure to pack him individually wrapped cookies or brownies. Pre-packaged junk food was currency in the first grade.

Except today, his mom announced they were out of brownies. Elliot tried to speed through his spelling but was still stuck in the back of the line with no bargaining chips. He promised double desserts the next day, but first graders sucked at understanding delayed gratification.

So Elliot was bouncing a basketball, hovering near the swings, his focus zeroed in, waiting for the moment one would open up. The teachers didn't allow kids to stand in front of the swings, so he had to pretend to be busy with "playing." No one understood that Elliot didn't know how to play. He only knew how to swing. Only felt the freedom from the stress of other kids not understanding him, of his teacher's disappointment that he didn't fit in, when he was in the beautiful ritual of leaning back, legs out; leaning forward, legs in; leaning back, legs out; leaning forward, legs in.

The basketball made its heavy *thud, thud, thud* on the asphalt as Elliot paced back and forth. He watched for even a micromovement from his classmates that would precede them getting off their swings.

His close attention was the only reason that he was already sprinting toward Damon as he launched himself into the air with a loud *yippee*. The excited yell was cut off by a pained scream as Damon landed hard, tumbling into the wood chips.

Elliot skidded to a stop in front of him, crouching down. His heart raced, and a tingling heat prickled along his arms.

"Ouch," Damon said, wincing as he cradled his arm. "That hurt."

"That was stupid," Elliot said.

"Yeah, but it was fun," Damon said, his eyes filling with tears.

Elliot didn't know why he did it, what part of his inner psyche woke up and raged at seeing someone hurt. No, not just someone, but *this* boy. He placed both of his hands on Damon's upper arm. There was a heavy energy, dense and cracked, but Elliot sensed he could massage it away. Not with his fingers, which rested gently on Damon's arm, but with the weird tingling heat that had flooded his limbs and seemed to originate from his core.

"What are you..." Damon stared at his arm.

Elliot focused his attention, his energy, and he imagined white light surrounding Damon's cracked arm bone.

Damon gasped.

Elliot removed his hand when the energy shifted. He blew out a breath and sat back on his feet.

Damon's warm brown skin was slightly damp from sweat that had gathered along the hairline of his short, tight curls. His dark eyes searched Elliot's face and then glanced at his arm in wonder. He twisted his shoulder, his wrist, and shook out his arm.

"What happened? Damon, I've told you repeatedly not to jump off the swings," Ms. Garlande said as she and the other teachers circled the boys.

"Sorry, Ms. G," Damon said, his eyes still locked on Elliot.

"Elliot, can you take Damon to the nurse?" Ms. Garlande asked.

Elliot nodded and stood, offering his hand to Damon.

Damon took Elliot's hand with his "bad" arm. The teachers returned to their posts once it was clear there wasn't a serious injury.

Elliot braced himself for Damon's questioning. What had he done to him? Why didn't his arm hurt anymore?

But Damon didn't grill him. He only smiled.

"You're a mess," Elliot said. He reached up and pulled a wood chip from Damon's shirt. He didn't know why he was blushing as he did it.

Damon shook like a dog to get the rest of the wood chips off. Elliot laughed as Damon grinned. "But my jump was pretty epic, right?"

Elliot shook his head, unable to contain the weird, fizzy lightness spreading through his chest. "Yeah, Damon. It was epic."

The boys walked off the playground. All eight swings occupied by their classmates. It was the first day Elliot could remember that he didn't care he wasn't one of them.

Chapter One

Senior Year of High School

"Stop!" Elliot laughed. "No, I hate it. Stop!" Elliot giggled like a little girl, which only encouraged Damon to continue tickling him.

"No! I'm not going to stop until you admit that I'm right," Damon said.

"Fuck you, Montré." Elliot pushed his shoulders, but Damon's quick hands found his ticklish sides again.

"Come on, Croft," Damon said, dodging Elliot's knee as it attempted to kick him in the nose. "Admit it. Say it!"

"No! Never!"

Damon made a weird growling noise in the back of his throat and launched himself on top of Elliot, flattening him to the carpet in Damon's bedroom. He pinned Elliot's arms over his head, straddling him. Damon's chest expanded and contracted in heavy pants.

Damon's brown eyes glittered with a bright animation that Elliot knew he'd never be able to conjure for himself.

"Admit it," Damon huffed, his breath falling over Elliot's face. It should have helped diffuse the predicament Elliot was currently in that Damon's breath smelled like nacho cheese and soda.

And yet, it didn't.

Elliot screwed his eyes shut as the parts of his body that were rubbing on his best friend started to perk up. He jerked around, twisting his body left and right in an attempt to wiggle out of Damon's hold, but Damon was stronger. He was the baseball team's star hitter. With his beefy biceps and wide shoulders, Damon could overpower Elliot whenever he wanted.

Elliot groaned inwardly. He shouldn't have *liked* that as much as he did. He turned his face toward the carpet to give himself enough time to mumble a spell under his breath.

By the power of Eros, hide my lust, conceal the truth before I bust.

Not the prettiest spell, but it came in handy when needing to a hide a boner from your best friend.

The spell redirected the blood from his lower body, not entirely, but it bought Elliot a little more time.

As a healing witch, he could manipulate the biomechanical functions of the body. Not very well, mind you. His grandmama could heal people who were in fatal car wrecks and have them walk away without a scrape.

Not Elliot. He usually choked when the people who were counting on him needed him the most.

He didn't have control over his secret powers, so he used spells to align his intentions. If he'd been better at magic, maybe he could've found an anti-boner spell, so he didn't have to ever worry about this particular situation.

Alas, he had not.

"Say it!" Damon demanded, and since he couldn't tickle Elliot while also pinning his arms over his head, he leaned down and pressed his face into Elliot's sides, tickling him with his nose.

Yeah, the spell was definitely not going to be enough. Not with Damon's mouth so close to his junk.

"Fine!" Elliot said. "I'll say it, if you get off me."

Damon grinned and rolled off.

Elliot took his time sitting up and fixing his shirt. He flipped his head to flick his long blonde hair out of his eyes. He felt Damon watching him with rapt anticipation. With a heavy sigh, Elliot said, "I'm just as good looking as you, and girls would like me if I actually talked to them."

Damon pushed his shoulder. "That's fucking right, Croft."

Elliot rolled his eyes. "Are you happy now?"

"Ecstatic, Elliot. I'm ecstatic." Damon threw an arm around his shoulders and leaned in, his mouth against Elliot's ear. "But if you really wanna make me happy, you'd believe it."

Elliot's breath stuttered, and he tried to shove Damon away, but Damon only tightened his arm and put him in a headlock, ruffling his hair.

"Ugh! You said you'd stop, dude!" Elliot said.

"Sorry," Damon said and resumed sitting beside him. "I just hate seeing you all upset. Need to snap you out of it."

Elliot picked up the game controller. "I'm not upset."

Yes, he was.

Damon was going to prom with Chelsea, who was undeniably the prettiest girl in school, and since it took Elliot by surprised, he'd been unable to muster the proper level of fake enthusiasm for his best friend.

Damon's ex-girlfriend Rochelle broke up with him a few weeks ago, so Elliot assumed neither he nor Damon were going to senior prom. He assumed that he wouldn't have to fake his smile while some girl danced with Damon, touched him, pressed up on him all night.

But when Damon asked Elliot why he was upset, Elliot couldn't very well tell him the truth, so he made a grumbling remark about how it was hard to be friends with someone who was at least three levels hotter than him.

Which prompted Damon's demand for Elliot to admit he was just as attractive as him and the only reason Elliot didn't get attention from girls was simply because he was shy.

It was true. He *was* shy.

And with his acne scars on pasty-white skin, too-long hair, and clothes that were always somehow too big or too short for his gangly limbs, it was also true that he was most definitely three or more levels below Damon in the looks department. What with Damon's perfect brown skin, twice-a-month barbershop appointments, and body that filled out his baseball uniform in ways that made Elliot's mouth go dry.

But despite the shyness and his unremarkable appearance, Elliot knew his lack of female attention probably had more to do with the fact that he was extremely gay.

Elliot was pretty sure the rest of the school knew, or at least sensed, he wasn't into girls, but since Elliot couldn't deny Damon anything, he agreed to ask out Damon's prom date's best friend just because Damon wanted them all to go to prom together as a group.

"Yeah, you're totally upset," Damon said. "I know you, Elliot. It's okay to be shy, but you gotta take a risk every once in a while." He grabbed the other controller and sat close enough to Elliot that their shoulders pressed together.

It wasn't because Damon wanted to touch him. He just had no boundaries. None whatsoever. That was never more obvious than after the thing that happened on spring break.

The thing Elliot tried really hard to *never* think about.

They were just best friends. They'd been like this since the day Damon broke his arm jumping off the swing and Elliot accidentally healed it, thereby cementing their friendship for eternity.

"Yeah, I guess I'm a little jealous," Elliot said. "But I'll get over it."

Jealous of Chelsea for getting to go to prom with *you*.

Damon snorted and proceeded to obliterate Elliot's character on the screen. Just like he obliterated Elliot's heart.

Every. Single. Day.

Chapter Two

"Is Elliot going to ask Madison out soon?" Chelsea asked as she chomped on a carrot stick next to Damon in the lunchroom.

Damon shrugged. "He hasn't said."

"Well, maybe you should ask him."

Damon sighed. Chelsea wasn't his girlfriend, but they'd been hooking up for the past two weeks. It was her idea to get Elliot and her best friend Madison to go to prom together since Madison was newly single. Damon thought it was a brilliant plan. He didn't want to go to prom without Elliot.

But Elliot was dragging his feet on the asking part.

"I mean..." Damon paused to chug his carton of milk. "Elliot already said he'd go with her, and Madison already said she'd go with him. Why does he have to ask her?"

Damon opened his second carton of milk. His coach said he needed more protein, and since his mom refused to buy the protein mixes all the other guys had, he had to get his protein from "whole foods."

Chelsea rubbed her eyes. "*Because* Damon, Madison agreed to this on the condition that Elliot would ask her in a very public manner to make Jason jealous."

Damon narrowed his eyes and put down his milk. "Wait. You did not tell me that."

"Yes, I did."

"No, pretty sure you didn't."

"I did," Chelsea said. "Remember when you were on the phone with Elliot the day I came over to your house? I reminded you to remind him about Madison."

"Yeah. Which I did."

"And I told you to tell him to make it a public asking out to make Jason jealous."

Damon's jaw worked. He definitely didn't remember her telling him this...

Or if she did, he wasn't paying attention.

If Damon was on the phone with Elliot when Chelsea said this, then yeah, he probably *wasn't* paying attention.

Elliot didn't call Damon much. He preferred texting and hated being on camera, which meant when Damon saw the incoming video call brighten his phone—with a shitty picture he'd taken of Elliot when he fell asleep and Damon put his long hair into pigtails—it'd felt sacred. Damon's stomach had flipped.

Because, you know, it was probably an emergency if he was calling.

It hadn't been an emergency. Or, at least, not something that Damon would classify as an emergency. Elliot, however, probably did think it was.

Elliot couldn't find his house keys, and one of his parents didn't put the spare key back under the frog statue after the last time they used it.

And what do you know? *Somehow,* his keys were in Damon's backpack.

He told Elliot he had *no* idea how they got there.

But, *of course*, Elliot could come over to get them.

Damon spent the next fifteen minutes trying to come up with a plan to get Chelsea to leave without pissing her off because if Elliot was coming over, Damon could probably convince him to play a game of Wizard Combat Zone 2.

And one game would turn into two, then Damon's mom would call them for dinner, and Elliot would have been tricked into hanging out with Damon even though he'd told him that he had to "study."

So yeah. Damon was distracted when Chelsea was explaining the details, thinking about his *tricking Elliot into hanging out* plan.

"Chelsea," Damon said. "There is no way Elliot is going to go for this. He's too...you know."

Chelsea pursed her lips. "I know. It probably wouldn't even work. Jason isn't going to be jealous of a gay guy asking Madison out, but I thought since Elliot hasn't officially come out that we could probably spread a rumor that he was bi and—"

"What?!" Damon put his carton of milk down too hard, and it splashed all over his tray.

Chelsea threw her hands up. "Don't worry! We were going to ask Elliot first about spreading the rumor. I'd never do it without his permission. Madison was going to ask after he asked her out, but he hasn't, so..."

"Elliot isn't gay."

Chelsea furrowed her brows. "So he *is* bi? That's even better! It's not a rumor."

Damon shook his head and stood up. He didn't know where he was going. "Elliot isn't...he isn't..." His palms were sweating. He sat back down, wiping his hands on his jeans. "Who told you he was gay?"

Chelsea's head jutted back. "Well...I..."

"Who was it? Who the fuck was it?" Damon didn't usually get angry, but his blood was burning. The asshole who'd spread this rumor was about to get his lights knocked out.

She shrugged. "I don't know who told me. I didn't think it was, like, a secret. I mean, no one talks about it or anything, but it's...I mean, you even said it."

Damon's face scrunched up. He finally understood the expression of seeing red. "What are you talking about?" he bit out.

She threw her hand out. "You said that Elliot won't ask Madison out publicly because he's *you know*."

"Shy, Chelsea," Damon said. "He's shy. That's what I was getting at."

"Oh." She looked down at her tray. "I'm sorry. I didn't know it was going to upset you."

"I don't like that you and the rest of the school are talking behind his back."

"I don't think anyone is, like, talking behind his back. It's just, like, one of those things. The sky is blue. The meatball subs in the cafeteria are not real meat. Elliot is gay." She shrugged. "I've never heard anyone make fun of him if that makes it better."

Damon put his tongue into his upper lip. He searched the cafeteria for the familiar sight of Elliot's floppy golden hair even though Damon knew Elliot didn't have lunch this period, and in fact, he was in calculus right now.

Elliot had history next, which meant they wouldn't cross paths because Damon's class was in the opposite direction. If he hurried, he could get there as class let out and—

"Damon?" Chelsea asked, her voice tiny.

"What?"

"Are you mad at me?"

"No," he said, but his tone didn't match his answer. "I just—I have to go." He got up and took his tray with him, tossing the rest of his lunch.

"Damon! Don't forget to remind Elliot to do the *thing*!" Chelsea yelled before he pushed the double doors and practically sprinted down the hall.

Chapter Three

"Hey," Elliot said as he walked out of calculus. Damon saddled up beside him. "Aren't you supposed to be in English?"

Yes, Elliot knew Damon's entire schedule by heart.

Yes, he realized he was obsessed with him to a more-than-friend degree.

"Yeah," Damon said. He wrung his hands and looked around the hall with a wild, frantic look in his eyes. "But I need to...I need to talk to you."

"Now? Ms. Benson will chew you out if you're late." Elliot furrowed his brows as he got to his locker and exchanged his books.

"Is this because I didn't ask Madison out yet?" Elliot sighed. "I just... I don't know. We both already know we're going together. Do I really have to ask her?"

Damon shook his head. "It's not about that."

"Okay..."

One of Damon's baseball teammates slapped him on the back in a passing greeting. Damon forced a smile at them as they walked away. "Maybe here isn't the best place."

"Dude," Elliot said. "What the fuck is going on?"

Damon was so easygoing. This was incredibly unsettling. He had two modes: happy and bouncing-off-the-walls excited. The only time Elliot had ever seen him outside of those two emotions had been when Damon's dad died in a car accident.

Elliot's stomach plummeted like it always did when he thought of that day, about his failure, about Damon's despair.

"Can you be late for your next class?" Damon asked.

He was officially scaring him. Had something terrible happened?

"Yeah," Elliot said. "What's going on? Is it your mom? Is she okay?"

He tried to recite the spell he used to calm his panic. *Don't take the bait, decrease my heart rate.*

Except, like usual, his magic didn't work when he really needed it, and Elliot spent the next thirty seconds spiraling out as Damon pulled him by the arm to the restroom.

Was his mom sick, or was he sick? *Oh god.* What if Damon was dying? If Elliot was better at healing magic, maybe he could do something. Maybe he could get his grandmama to help. Maybe it wasn't too late—

"She's fine. Everyone's fine," Damon said.

Elliot exhaled.

Damon released him once they were in the restroom. He did the thing they do in the movies where they kick open all the stalls to make sure they were alone.

The bell rang, echoing in the empty tiled bathroom. They were officially late.

Damon whipped around, glanced at the door behind him, and then whispered, "Are you gay?"

Elliot froze, muscles tensing like an animal caught in the crosshairs. His hands tingled, the magic in him trying to escape, to heal something and dissipate the fight-or-flight response bubbling inside of him.

Damon's eyes darted around his face, searching for the answer, since Elliot couldn't find his voice. "You can tell me, Elliot. Just...You can tell me anything. I'm your best friend."

Elliot hung his head, staring toward the floor but not really seeing anything.

This wasn't how he'd fantasized coming out to Damon. He imagined one day he'd gather the courage to say, *I'm gay, Damon, and I want to be with you in a way that is more than friendly*. At first, Damon would be taken aback, but then he'd smile his usual smile and grab Elliot and pull him close, and Damon's lips would find his and—

"Elliot?"

Elliot blinked away the fantasy. He took a deep breath. "Yeah. I'm gay, okay?"

Damon's face crumbled, and he grabbed his stomach like he'd taken a punch to the gut.

Elliot had imagined a lot of worst-case scenarios to admitting his sexuality, but Damon being disgusted hadn't been one of them. Damon had never made homophobic comments, had never shown any signs that he might be upset with his best friend liking men.

Elliot focused on the little rectangle window high above the stalls. He wasn't very tall. It was unlikely he'd be able to crawl out of here. He'd need a lift to reach it.

And wasn't that what was truly fucked? Elliot couldn't even imagine an escape plan that didn't involve Damon's help.

Damon stepped sideways, blocking Elliot's view of the window. "I'm not judging you. I don't care if you're gay." He reached out a hand to grab Elliot's shoulder but then pulled it back.

Elliot scoffed to hide the fact his insides were being shredded into pieces. "Yeah, okay, Damon. Is that it? Can I go to class?"

Damon ran a hand down his face. "Elliot. Why are you...? Why didn't you tell me? Chelsea had to tell me."

Elliot pursed his lips. "How did Chelsea know?"

He shrugged. "She said she just knew. That everyone knows. Everyone except me, I guess." He leaned on the sink. "Why, Elliot? Why'd you let me go on and on about hooking you up with girls and all that bullshit?"

Elliot sighed. "What does it matter? It's not like I'm going to date anyone."

"Why?"

"Why what?"

"Why can't you date guys?"

"You mean all the guys who are interested in dating a skinny-ass nerd like me? Oh, wait." Elliot snapped. "There are none of those."

Damon rubbed his palm over his chin. "I'm sure there are guys in our school who are gay too. I'm sure—"

Elliot snorted. "Oh, there are. That's not the problem. I've fucked around with them, but they aren't interested in *dating*."

Damon's eye twitched.

Elliot's cheeks heated. Damon had never been shy about sharing his hookup history, but apparently the thought of Elliot messing around with guys was too much.

Damon made a helpless noise, shaking his head in disbelief. "It's like I don't even know you. You know everything about me. And you have this whole other life that you've kept from me."

Elliot threw his arms up. "I'm allowed to have things I keep to myself! Just because you want to describe in excruciating detail the way pussy tastes doesn't mean I have to return the favor."

Damon's eyebrows pulled down as sadness deflated his features.

Regret pitted Elliot's stomach. It wasn't true. He wanted to know every single detail about Damon, even the parts that made him burn with jealousy, but he couldn't take it back now. He turned on his heel and said over his shoulder, "I have to go to class."

Damon didn't stop him.

Chapter Four

Damon and Elliot had gotten into fights before. When they were younger, it was usually because Damon didn't understand why Elliot insisted on doing things a certain way. Damon's mom had to explain to him that some people were extra sensitive.

That the things Damon loved about Elliot—his kindness and understanding, his quiet reassuring presence—those things came from that sensitivity.

Elliot always knew Damon's feelings without Damon ever having to explain them. He was the calming presence that held Damon as he broke down when his dad died. Damon wouldn't have gotten through that time without him.

But that sensitivity meant Elliot usually avoided conflict. He let the things that bothered him fester under the surface until he exploded and it ended up in a huge fight that Damon didn't see coming.

Damon knew this. He tried to be better. Tried to be more sensitive, like his best friend.

But he never really mastered that preternatural way Elliot just knew things about him. About when he was scared or sad. When he needed space or needed comfort. When he was about to do something stupid and needed to be talked out of jumping off swings or roofs.

Damon could see that every fight they'd had in the last four years had been because Damon was pushing Elliot to date or trying to set him up.

It made sense now why Elliot had shut down when Damon told him about going to prom with Chelsea. Why his shoulders had hunched and he wouldn't meet Damon's eye as he explained how Elliot and Madison could go together to the dance. Elliot wasn't jealous of Damon at all. He was sick of Damon pressuring him into being someone he wasn't.

Damon rubbed his eyes. It made him sick to remember everything he'd said to him. The hours and hours he went on, trying to coach him on how to talk to girls or how they liked to be kissed or touched. It never occurred to him that Elliot might be gay. Damon thought he was just shy and needed advice.

God, he was such a dick.

Everyone in school knew, or assumed, that Elliot was gay, but Damon didn't see it. Didn't know his best friend at all.

Elliot was his everything, and he kept this from Damon, which meant Damon wasn't as important to Elliot as Elliot was to him.

It'd been a week since he'd hauled Elliot into the restrooms and basically forced him to come out.

Damon tried, multiple times, to type out an apology text, but everything sounded stupid. He scrolled through their text thread. The last message was ten days ago. Elliot reminding him that Damon's mom's birthday was this week. Or last week. Which Damon had forgotten anyway because he was a terrible person. Elliot probably would have reminded him again on the day of if they weren't still fighting.

He deleted his pathetic *I'm sorry* text and left his phone in his bedroom. He went down the stairs and into the kitchen to deliver the other apology he owed.

"Hey, Momma?"

"Hmm?" his mom said, stirring something in a pot.

"Can I help you with dinner?"

She looked up and smiled. "Sure, baby. That'd be great. You want to get stuff out for the salad? Cut up the veggies?"

Damon opened the fridge. "Uh, so," he started, grabbing the veggies. "I'm really sorry I forgot to say happy birthday the other day. I suck."

His mom laughed. "It's okay, hun. I know you have a lot on your mind with semifinals coming up."

He deposited all the vegetables on the counter and went to his mom, hugging her from behind. "Still. I'm sorry, Momma. Happy late birthday."

She patted his hand. "Thank you, Damon."

"Should we go out to eat or something this weekend? My treat?"

Turning to him, she smiled and said, "Yeah, that'd be nice."

"We could go to the restaurant you and Dad always went to."

"I think I'd like that."

Damon grabbed a knife and started cutting the vegetables. It'd taken years for them to finally be able to talk about his dad without tears.

The night of the car crash was the worst of his life. It'd been after Elliot and Damon's sixth-grade graduation. Damon's parents had taken them both to a gaming arcade to celebrate. A drunk driver swerved into their lane.

His mom had a broken pelvis and almost lost her ability to walk. Damon and Elliot got away with nothing but a couple cuts, even though Elliot had been on the driver's side in the backseat.

No one understood how he hadn't died. That side of the car was completely smashed in.

No one understood a lot about that day. Like how Elliot, at twelve years old, had been able to get Damon's dad out of the totaled car.

The image of the paramedics carrying a kicking-and-screaming Elliot away from Damon's dad's body was seared into his brain. Elliot kept fighting them and shouting about how he could save him, how he could fix him.

All Damon did was stand there. He didn't even try to help. He didn't even check on his mom.

Elliot had been the one to shake him out of it. He'd wrapped his arms around Damon and apologized over and over. It'd made Damon feel so guilty that, in that moment, he was capable of feeling okay. That he felt better because his best friend was holding him.

How could anyone feel okay standing only a couple of feet away from their dead father?

But Elliot always made Damon feel better. No matter what was happening.

A broken arm.

A broken heart.

Elliot could always fix it, or at least, make it easier to bear.

"We can invite Elliot too," Damon's mom said. "I haven't seen him around in a few days?"

It was her subtle way of saying she knew he was moping around.

"We got into a fight."

"About what?"

Damon sighed, cutting the tomato with a gentle hand. Was he supposed to keep it a secret? Had Elliot told his parents?

Damon worried his lip. "I found out a secret he'd been keeping from me. Kinda forced him to tell me. I don't think I reacted the right way, and I don't know how to apologize for forcing him to tell me when I feel like crap that he didn't tell me in the first place."

His mom made a humming noise. "Elliot is a private person," she said. "Remember how it took him two years before he could answer a question at the dinner table without blushing and stuttering?"

Damon smiled. He'd forgotten about that. Elliot had been so nervous around his parents. Around any authority figure really. He hated the first day of school because he didn't know how the teacher would expect him to behave.

"I thought that I was different," Damon said. "I thought we didn't keep secrets from each other."

Damon's mom turned off the stove and put a hand on his arm. "I'm sure he wished he could tell you but was scared. Whatever it was, it was probably hard for him to talk about."

After they finished having dinner, Damon tried again to type out an apology, but he quickly gave up.

It was probably better if he did it in person, anyway.

Chelsea mentioned at lunch that she'd talked to Elliot about asking Madison to prom. Damon had hummed distractedly at first, and then tried to grill her about what else she talked about with him.

She'd gone into great detail about the plan she'd made for Elliot's prom-posal. Damon spaced out when he realized she wasn't going to tell him anything *Elliot* had said.

He probably should have paid more attention to Chelsea's prom-posal plan so he wouldn't have been so surprised by the scene he stumbled upon as he turned the corner of the hall.

A crowd gathered around Madison's locker. There were origami hearts taped to the outside. She plucked an envelope off the locker and cleared her throat, loud enough that everyone in the hall could hear her.

"Madison," she read. "Your beauty distracted me all through our lesson on differential equations, but I won't be upset that you got a better grade than me on our last exam if you go to prom with me?"

Damon rolled his eyes. Elliot most certainly didn't get distracted by Madison's beauty. Sure, Madison was pretty, but even if he hadn't known Elliot wasn't into girls, he'd know that this was fake because Elliot didn't get distracted in class.

He never, *ever*, let anyone or anything come between him and a good grade.

If Madison did get a better grade than he did on his last exam, it was probably the day after Damon stole Elliot's keys and convinced him to stay over instead of studying.

Now that Damon thought about it, maybe Elliot was better off without him.

The crowd parted, and Elliot stood, smiling and leaning near the vestibule with the water fountains.

He was wearing his usual jeans and beat-up sneakers, but had on a tight red t-shirt that Damon had never seen him wear before. It emphasized his lean frame and gave him a more styled and put-together look. He'd also gotten a haircut so his long blonde hair didn't cover his blue eyes.

He looked good. Really good. Damon didn't understand why anyone wouldn't want to date Elliot. Why he only *fucked around* with guys. Why anyone wouldn't want to shout to the world that this sweet, kind, cute guy was his—

"Yes, I'll go to prom with you!" Madison screamed louder than necessary. She ran over with her arms wide. Elliot met her halfway and pulled her in close. He hugged her and spun her around, smiling like he...actually liked her or something.

Why was Elliot even asking her to prom? He was only supposed to go with Madison so he could hang out with *Damon*. It was supposed to be their last senior-year hurrah. They were going to sneak in a flask and have a good time together.

Damon didn't even want to go to prom anymore. It wouldn't be fun without Elliot.

The crowd was still clapping for the happy couple.

Madison grabbed both sides of Elliot's face and kissed him.

Damon expected him to freeze up or push her away, but instead, he didn't hesitate to kiss her back.

The crowd's clapping turned into whistling.

Damon clenched his hands into fists. His chest burned. He wanted to punch something, and he had no idea why.

Chapter Five

"If you can't get the hang of this, Elliot, I'll bind your powers."

He sighed. "Yes, Grandmama." He wanted to fling his hands out and say *Just bind them. I don't want them anyway. It's not like they work when it actually matters.*

Elliot hovered his hands over the sedated dog lying on the vet table in his grandmama's clinic. He'd been helping out here since he was a kid. Since the first time his powers manifested.

That fateful day in first grade when he'd healed a broken arm.

Healing witches were a family legacy on his dad's side. Everyone had been excited that Elliot's powers had manifested early because it was a sign he'd be extremely powerful once his powers matured on his eighteenth birthday.

Elliot, however, had been a disappointment.

His powers were erratic and unreliable. He'd turned eighteen three months ago and couldn't even heal this dog's broken leg.

"Maybe if you were a certain ridiculously reckless guy, I could heal you," he mumbled to the dog.

But every time Elliot wanted to give up, to accept that his powers must have skipped him like they had his dad, he remembered the car crash.

Remembered how his healing powers had saved him from almost dying. Had jumped from his skin to save Damon too.

They hadn't been enough to save Damon's father. Damon would have a dad if Elliot weren't such a shitty witch.

Elliot's grandmama huffed after another five minutes passed and nothing happened. She waved a hand over the dog, and the bone and skin knitted itself back together.

"I'm sorry," Elliot said, energy deflating. "I don't know why I can't do it."

"You aren't focused. Where's your mind?"

Elliot wrinkled his nose, shrugging.

Grandmama hobbled over to the bench in the corner and slumped into the seat. She was paler than usual. Her normally mischievous eyes were tired and sunken. A lethargy hung heavy in her aura.

She looked like she had after she'd healed Damon's mom's broken pelvis after the crash. It'd taken weeks for her to recover after healing an injury of that extent.

"Are you okay?" Elliot asked.

"I'm fine. Just old. We had a hoarder situation earlier today. Healing eleven animals at one time might have overworked my powers a little."

Elliot worried his lip. Another reason he needed to learn to summon his magic at will so he could take some of the burden off her shoulders. "You need to be careful. One of these days you're going to burnout or have a heart attack or something."

Grandmama waved a dismissive hand. "You should know better than to lecture me, boy. I *will* bind your powers."

Elliot rolled his eyes and plopped down on the doctor stool.

Grandmama would never. She was just stubborn and prideful.

That stubbornness was why she still hadn't given up on Elliot. For some reason, she still believed in him.

"I can tell your mind is elsewhere," she said, refusing to take the hint that Elliot didn't want to talk about it.

"Damon and I got into a fight," he finally admitted.

She stared, waiting for him to continue.

"Apparently a girl in our school told him I was gay. He asked me, and I couldn't lie to his face."

Grandmama was the only person in his family that he'd come out to. It wasn't that he thought his parents wouldn't accept him, more that he just didn't see the point. It's not like he had a boyfriend or anything.

"He didn't react well?"

Elliot gave a one-shoulder shrug. "He was upset." After replaying the conversation in his head over and over, Elliot realized that Damon wasn't being homophobic or rejecting him. "He was hurt that I didn't tell him."

Guilt gnawed at him every time he saw Damon in the hall, every time he thought about texting him, because being gay wasn't the only secret he was keeping from him.

Elliot had wanted to tell Damon he was a witch for years, but if he did, he'd have to own up to the fact that it was his fault that Damon's dad was dead. Elliot was a coward, too afraid of losing his best friend, so he kept his powers a secret too.

Grandmama hummed. "That boy has always been strangely possessive of you."

"No, he hasn't."

She raised her eyebrows.

"He isn't," Elliot insisted.

"Okay."

Elliot spun himself around on the doctor stool, staring at the ceiling. "I feel like crap that I'm keeping so many secrets from him, but now that he knows I like guys, it's only a matter of time until he figures out how I feel about him."

"When was the last time your powers worked?" Grandmama asked.

Elliot sighed and stopped spinning on the chair. Guess they were done talking about Damon. That was fine. He hadn't wanted to talk about him, anyway. "I don't know. Like maybe over the summer? Or no, Christmas break. I was able to heal myself when I cut my finger." Elliot wasn't about to tell her about his boner-reducing spells.

Grandmama squinted. "You cut yourself at Damon's house."

"Yeah, we were helping his mom with dinner."

She pursed her lips. "And before that, in the summer, what happened?"

Elliot narrowed his eyes, thinking. "I healed that dog who got run over by the car, remember? The one with the ruptured spleen?"

"And earlier that day you were with Damon?"

Elliot rolled his lips. "Uh huh." He remembered that day vividly. They'd been invited to a pool party, which devolved into a game of chicken. Damon had lifted Elliot onto his shoulders. His big hands had wrapped around Elliot's thighs and squeezed them to keep him steady.

After their team won, Damon had been elated. He'd tossed Elliot over his shoulder like he weighed nothing. Damon ran around the pool, shouting their victory. He'd slapped his ass—in a very manly, platonic *dudes in sports* kind of way—but Elliot's body didn't recognize the platonic part. When Damon finally put him down, Elliot's body slid across his best friend's wet, naked chest in torturous slow motion.

Elliot had to excuse himself because his lust-killing spell was not working, and in fact, his powers were churning in his veins, heating him from the inside out.

By the time he finally got them under control, his shift at the clinic was in an hour and he had to leave.

"The first time your powers manifested, it was because Damon was hurt," Grandmama said. "He's the key. Your powers react to him."

"What?" Elliot asked. "No one else's powers work like that."

She shrugged. "Prove me wrong. Go make up with him and come back here. I bet your powers are jumping from your skin."

Elliot shook his head. "I spend like every day with him. If he was the key, why don't my powers work every day?"

Grandmama pinched the bridge of her nose, looking put upon. "Because I'm guessing that there is a very specific energy that you're tapping into with him on certain days?"

Elliot blushed. His grandmama wasn't really saying he needed to be horny to get his powers to work, was she? Horny for Damon because his powers certainly didn't get boosted when he messed around in the backseat of his car with guys from school.

"Give it a shot. Let me know if it works." Grandmama said. "But keep the details to yourself."

Yep. That was exactly what she was saying.

Elliot had been a wreck for the past week and a half. He missed Damon so much. Going to his house. Sitting on his bed. Just being near him.

He couldn't live this way anymore. He needed Damon in his life, and he didn't want to hide who he was.

Damon already knew he was gay, so telling him that Elliot was a witch probably couldn't be much harder...

And then Elliot could hang out with Damon again and know that he'd told his best friend all of his secrets.

Well, almost all of his secrets.

All of the secrets that actually mattered.

Elliot stayed after school on Thursday and settled himself on the uncomfortable metal bleachers outside the baseball field. It didn't take long to find Damon. Elliot's eyes were magnetized to the long graceful lines of his body and the rippling of his muscled arms as he threw the ball to his teammates in the outfield.

The clouds parted, and the sun shined down on Damon like he was an angel. His brown skin glistened. His every movement, divine.

Elliot left his bag on the bleachers and walked toward the chain-link fence to get a closer look. Parents and other adults lined the edges, talking to their kids before the game.

He didn't know how Damon knew that Elliot was there, but Damon turned and looked straight at him.

Elliot held his breath.

Damon grinned, and he tossed the ball to someone and jogged over.

Elliot hooked his fingers into the chain-link fence and pressed himself as close as possible. Being in Damon's sightline made something inside of him feel lighter, his magic fizzing in his veins.

Damon pulled his glove off and tossed it on the ground. He grabbed the chain-link fence on his side, his hands just inches away from Elliot's.

"What are you doing here?" Damon asked, out of breath, despite only jogging a few yards.

"I haven't missed a single game in four years. Not gonna start now," Elliot answered, his voice low and husky.

Damon's eyebrows pulled together in gratitude. He nodded like a bobblehead. "No. You never have. You're like my biggest fan." His face fell. "Or...well, I guess, you were...before I fucked up—"

Elliot wasn't thinking when he released the chain-link fence and threaded his fingers through the metal that Damon grabbed, effectively holding his hand from the other side.

"I'll always be your biggest fan, Damon."

Damon's bottom lip trembled; his dark eyes became intense, searching, probing.

The corner of Elliot's mouth quirked up. It wasn't often he could leave Damon speechless.

Damon's throat worked in a hard swallow. "I'm so sorry for—" He glanced around at the people surrounding them. Elliot expected him to pull his hand away, but he didn't. "I'm sorry for forcing you to tell me your secret. You were right. I'm not entitled to know everything. You deserve privacy, and I'm sorry. So sorry. I'm *your* biggest fan, Elliot. Always."

Damon moved his other hand—the one that Elliot wasn't holding—and he threaded his fingers over top of Elliot's free hand.

His stomach swooped. At some point, their faces had gotten closer to the chain-link fence. They'd be close enough to kiss if the metal wasn't in the way.

A whistle blew, and they startled. Damon turned toward the dugouts, and Elliot reluctantly stepped back, pulling his hands away.

"It's okay, Montré," Elliot said. "Go knock 'em out of the park, yeah? I'm skipping studying to be here, so you better not let your biggest fan down."

Damon turned back to Elliot with a crooked grin. "You got it, Croft." He scooped up his discarded glove and jogged away.

Elliot tried (and failed) to not watch his ass in his tight baseball pants as he crossed the field.

Chapter Six

Damon was on fire tonight. Elliot had come to his game, and he'd forgiven him.

Damon had been super depressed at practice yesterday because he knew he'd walk up to the plate and look up to the normal spot that Elliot always sat and it'd be empty—or worse, someone else would be sitting there.

But his best friend was exactly where he was supposed to be.

And he had the perfect view to watch Damon hit the ball out of the park, just like Elliot had asked. Damon pointed up to the stands to let Elliot know that one was for him.

Elliot smiled and shook his head.

Damon went into the next inning confident that he could take his team to the finals for the third year in a row, but that feeling didn't last long because as Damon ran for the fly ball, he knew the second he collided, head first, with his teammate and hit the ground that neither of them had caught it.

His final thought before he blacked out was *Shit, Elliot's going to be so upset.*

The world was spinning, and his head throbbed. God, it hurt so fucking bad.

"Damon? Damon!"

He smiled when he heard Elliot's voice, or he tried to, but moving his face sent shooting pain through his head. "No worries. S'fine."

"You need to step back."

"Elliot. Get back. Let the paramedics do their job."

"Damon!" Elliot yelled. "No, come on. I can help him. I can—"

"S'okay, Elliot. I'm fine. Totally fine."

"Shh," a medic said. "Don't try to talk right now."

Damon tried to look around, to find Elliot, but his vision was spotty, and someone was holding his head in one place.

He didn't remember the trip to the hospital or any of the tests they did. He woke up to his mom hovering over his hospital bed.

When he was finally conscious and coherent, he croaked out, "Elliot?"

His mom ignored him and started crying and fussing over him.

"Mom. I'm fine. Where's Elliot?"

His mom sniffed, patting his arm. "I don't know."

"Where's my phone?"

"I don't know."

"Mom!"

"Damon. Please calm down. Here," she said. "Text him with mine."

Damon grabbed it and squinted at the phone. His head started pounding.

The doctor came in. "I don't recommend looking at screens until your concussion passes."

Damon's mom snatched the phone back.

"Concussion?" Damon asked. "How long will I be out?"

"Your concussion should clear up in two weeks, but your broken arm will take longer to heal."

"My what?" Damon said. He looked at his arms.

The doctor hung an x-ray film on the view box and turned on the backlight. "You have a fracture right here, see? We'll get you in a cast, but it'll be about eight weeks until it heals."

"You got the wrong x-rays, doc," Damon said. He wiggled both arms around in the air. "My arms are fine."

The doctor's eyebrows furrowed. He grabbed Damon's left arm and poked it, asking if it hurt. He rechecked the x-rays and mumbled something as he left.

Damon turned to his mom. "Can you please text Elliot? Tell him that I'm okay?"

Damon's mom nodded and texted him, but as the little *swoosh* of a sent text message filled the room, someone skidded to a stop outside his room.

"Elliot!" Damon said, smiling.

Elliot sighed out a relieved breath. He walked into the room and leaned down, wrapping his arms around Damon. "This hospital is a maze. They moved you twice since I got here," he mumbled.

Damon hummed and hugged him back. Nothing else mattered. Elliot was here. Everything was okay now.

"I'll leave you boys alone," Damon's mom said, walking out.

Damon nuzzled his nose into Elliot's neck, breathing in his crisp piney scent. His Elliot scent.

"I was so afraid," Elliot said. His forehead was pressed to Damon's shoulder. "It was like—"

Like the car accident, Damon knew he was about to say. He ran his hands up and down his back. "I'm okay. It's okay."

Elliot sniffed, and Damon became aware that his shirt was damp with tears.

"Hey," Damon said, pulling back. "I'm okay, really."

Elliot tried to smile.

Damon reached up and touched Elliot's cheeks, wiping under his eyes with his thumbs. "Don't cry over me, Croft."

"You passed out on the field, and they wouldn't let me near you, wouldn't let me help. I was so scared."

Elliot tilted his head into Damon's hand, and something twisted in Damon's chest.

"They wouldn't let you help, huh? What was your plan? Gonna give me CPR or something?" As soon as the words were out, Damon's eyes went wide. It would have been a joke he'd have made before he knew Elliot was gay, but now it felt wrong. Joking about Elliot's mouth on his. About the air in his lungs being breathed into Damon's lungs. About Elliot's hands on his face. Kinda like how Damon's were on Elliot's face right now...

Damon's stomach pitted. That anxious feeling in his gut—that was guilt, right? He didn't want to make Elliot uncomfortable.

Elliot didn't seem to notice Damon's inner crisis because he sniffed and stood straighter, face becoming somber. "I have to tell you something."

Damon nodded robotically and pulled his hand away. That feeling in his gut was definitely anxiety.

Elliot walked to the door and shut it before returning.

"Whoa. This is serious, huh?" Damon tried to joke.

Elliot sat on the edge of his bed. "This may come as a surprise to you, but promise me you'll keep it a secret, even if you don't believe what I say. You have to—" He swallowed. "You have to promise, no matter how crazy you think I am, that you won't tell anyone."

Damon didn't feel like making a joke anymore. "I promise. You can tell me anything."

Elliot fingered the sheets on the bed near Damon's hand. He didn't know why, but he wished Elliot would touch him, would hold his hand as he said whatever it was he wanted to say.

Elliot took a deep breath and released it. His eyes glided up to Damon's. "I'm a witch. I healed your broken arm in the first grade, and I healed the other one like forty-five minutes ago."

Chapter Seven

When Elliot watched Damon crash into his teammate on the baseball field, he almost had a heart attack. His chest ached so much that it threatened to bring him to his knees. He'd ignored the pain and ran onto the field, trying to push through the players and coaches and medics.

He wasn't quick enough. Someone grabbed him and held him back before he could get close enough to touch Damon and heal him.

Elliot watched, helpless, as they put him into the ambulance. Damon's eyes were closed, and his arm was bent in a sickening angle.

Elliot's magic burned through him, straining, reaching, yelling out for his best friend.

Elliot had ridden the bus that morning, so he didn't have his car. He called his mom and dad, but they were both slammed with work and couldn't drive him to the hospital.

His grandmama drove up to the baseball field twenty-five minutes later. She took one look at his hands, which were intermittently blinking white light, and said, "It's him, isn't it? He's the key to your magic."

Elliot could only nod. Too numb from shock. He got into the car and squeezed his hands together to get the magic to calm.

"What happened?" Grandmama finally asked after Elliot's heartbeat ratcheted down.

"I'm pretty sure his arm is broken," Elliot said. "I'm going to heal him. He's got a scholarship for baseball. An injury could make them revoke it."

Then they wouldn't go to college together.

Elliot was not going to let that happen.

Grandmama tapped her fingers on the steering wheel. "You do what you got to."

Grandmama never instilled fear into Elliot about sharing his power, not like the covens did, which was why Grandmama and Elliot were considered outcasts among them. She wanted to do more to help people, but the covens were too afraid of risking exposure.

The world they lived in was ruled by powerful drug companies who would defend the use of their expensive medicines until their last breaths. If entire industries could be toppled with a simple wave of a witch's hand? They'd be courting extinction, the covens warned.

So healing witches worked on the peripheral and didn't draw attention to themselves.

Elliot stared out the window, gnawing on his lip and thinking about his best friend. "And I already decided I'm going to tell him."

"That you're in love with him?"

"I'm not in *love* with him!" Elliot said. "It's just a little crush."

Grandmama hummed.

"But no. I'm not telling him that. I'm going to tell him I'm a witch. I can't keep secrets from him anymore." Damon deserved to know whose fault it was his dad was gone. Elliot shouldn't have kept it a secret for as long as he had.

"Seems a little contradictory," she said, and Elliot grimaced. "But you do what feels right."

"I'm a witch," Elliot said. "I healed your broken arm in the first grade, and I healed the other like forty-five minutes ago."

Damon just blinked. His long black eyelashes fanned his face. Even all disheveled and in a hospital gown, Damon was gorgeous. Elliot was entranced by the strong cut of his jaw and his plump lips with the little dip in the middle.

Elliot shook himself out of ogling his best friend and continued, "I healed us after the car crash. Accidentally. I don't really have control over my powers. I'm not good at them. I tried"—he hiccupped, tears blurring his vision again—"I tried to heal your dad, but it didn't work. I'm so sorry. I'm sorry for not telling you. For not being better. For not saving him."

Elliot sniffed and wiped his eyes, searching Damon's face for any clue that he believed him, or if Damon was about to punch him in the face.

But Damon kept blinking.

Maybe Elliot broke him.

Damon finally took a long inhale and sighed it out. His fingers intertwined with Elliot's. "The police report said Dad was dead on impact. No one could have saved him."

"No, no. I could have—I should have been able to—"

Damon squeezed his hand. "You may be a healing witch, Elliot, but you aren't a god. Unless you're about to tell me that you can do necromancy too?"

Elliot's jaw quivered. The disbelief over his casual acceptance was staggering. That he could *joke* about this.

Damon smiled, his eyes narrowing, and then he was nodding his head. "You know...this explains *so* much."

It was Elliot's turn to blink dumbly.

"So can you heal concussions too?" Damon asked. "Because my head hurts like a bitch."

Chapter Eight

Things between Elliot and Damon went back to normal.

Well, mostly normal.

Elliot was acting normal. Damon, however, was trying very hard to hide how weird he was acting, which only made him weirder.

On the bright side, Damon was pretty sure Elliot attributed his awkward behavior to Elliot's admission of being a witch...and not the *real* reason.

Part of Damon had suspected that Elliot did something to fix his arm after he'd jumped off the swing in first grade, but as Damon got older, he figured he'd misremembered how much pain he'd been in.

Elliot having healing powers just made sense. It explained his ability to always know how Damon was feeling and why his touch made everything better. Damon wasn't freaked out about it. He'd always known that Elliot was special.

No, that wasn't the revelation that was making Damon act weird.

"My mom wants to take us to get our suit rentals," Damon said, elbowing Elliot so he missed when he shot at Damon's team as they played Wizard Combat Zone 2.

"Okay," Elliot said, elbowing him back. "When?"

"I don't know. Next weekend?" Damon shoved his shoulder into Elliot's.

"Sure." He retaliated by kicking Damon's shin and killing his entire squad.

"Yes!" Elliot threw his arms up. "Sucker!"

Damon tossed his controller and dove toward him, wrapping his arms around Elliot's waist and taking him down.

"Omph."

"You kicked me," Damon complained. He buried his face into Elliot's stomach to tickle him and used all of his weight to wrestle him to the ground. "You cheated."

"You were shoving me first!"

Elliot tried to break away, but Damon used his legs to wrap around his and didn't let him escape.

Elliot panted. His blonde hair curtained one of his eyes. It grew too fast. It'd only been one week, and he already needed another haircut. Damon hated when Elliot's hair obscured the sight of his blue eyes.

"You're the cheater," Elliot said.

"No." Damon rolled them and pressed his body into Elliot, weighing him down, flattening him. Every inch of Elliot's body was covered by Damon's. Elliot went limp under him and stopped struggling.

Damon sat up, his hands on Elliot's shoulders to pin him, his legs on either side of his waist.

Elliot's eyes widened. It took Damon an embarrassingly long time to realize why Elliot was panicking.

"Shit," Damon said and rolled off in a clumsy panic. "Sorry. I—"

"It's fine," he said, fixing his shirt and running a hand through his hair. "It's fine."

"I shouldn't have—"

"We always do—"

"Right, but that was before..."

Elliot met his eyes when he didn't finish the sentence. "Before you knew I was gay?"

Damon averted his gaze. "It's just...well, if I did that with a girl, I'd probably be getting turned on, and..." His gaze traveled from Elliot's bare feet, over the light dusting of hair on his legs, to the zipper on his pants. Was he hard? Did he make Elliot hard?

Why did that thought make something tug deep in Damon's stomach?

Elliot snorted. "You've got a high opinion of yourself, don't you?" He grabbed the controller and plopped down on the futon, starting a single-player game.

"What do you mean? I know you think I'm hot. I distinctly remember being told I was three levels hotter than you. Which I still think is bullshit, by the way."

"I have eyes and can see that you are attractive," he said. "Doesn't mean you're my type."

Damon didn't know why he was more than a little offended. He furrowed his brow and crossed his arms over his chest. "Are you saying I'm not?"

Elliot snorted again and glanced over quickly before settling his gaze on the screen. "What exactly do you want the answer to that question to be?"

Damon dropped his arms to his sides.

Elliot's gaze stayed glued to the TV while Damon's bounced all over him. Elliot flicked his head back to get his hair out of his eyes, and Damon's fingers twitched to grab the hair clip that he always put in his hair when it got this long, but if he did that now...

If Damon wrestled him to the floor and sat on him and ran his hands through his hair to clip it back, would Elliot think Damon was coming on to him?

Fuck. Had Damon been coming on to him this whole time?

No wonder Elliot never told him he was gay.

"We probably shouldn't be horsing around anyway," Elliot said. "Just because I healed your concussion doesn't mean you shouldn't be careful about jostling your tiny pea brain around more than necessary."

"Ha," he said. "Hilarious."

His heart raced, and his palms started sweating. Damon mumbled something about using the bathroom and practically sprinted down the hall.

He gripped either side of the sink and stared into the mirror. His face was flushed from wrestling with Elliot. "Do I like guys?" he whispered.

He shook his head. No way. He *really* liked boobs.

Like a fucking lot.

He'd never jerked it to a guy.

Although…sometimes he did notice good-looking guys.

But that was appreciation, right? He wanted to be them, not touch them.

Except he did like touching Elliot. He never touched any of his other friends like that. But Elliot was his best friend. It was different.

Damon stared into the mirror as if he could find the truth of his sexuality if he looked hard enough. His eyes caught on the swim trunks he'd hung on the shower rod to dry out.

Damon had way over paid for those trunks.

His mom had surprised him by letting him bring Elliot on their spring break vacation. It was a kind of joint eighteenth birthday gift to them both. Damon had turned eighteen in the fall, and Elliot's birthday had been the week before they left.

While his mom was out, doing whatever grown women do in the morning at the beach, Elliot and Damon slept in late.

The beach didn't get fun until the middle of the afternoon, so they were being lazy and spent the morning shooting the shit in bed.

They'd slept side-by-side, but it was a king-size bed. It wasn't like they were cuddling or anything. Besides Damon's mom was sleeping in the bed next to them. So that would have been weird.

And maybe because Damon didn't have any of his usual privacy, he was a little extra horny that morning, which was probably why he started going on about the logistics of threesomes.

"I think doing it standing would be the easiest," Damon had said. "If all three people are standing, then one guy could be in front and one in the back."

"As long as the guys are the same height," Elliot said.

"The taller guy could crouch to get it in," Damon said.

"Yeah, but that's like uncomfortable and annoying. Like thrusting would be…" Elliot squinted his eyes and thrust his hips up off the bed like he was trying to picture the angle.

"Yeah," Damon said. "But you're having a threesome, so who cares if it's a little uncomfortable?"

"You want to have a threesome with another guy?"

Damon shrugged. "Yeah, why not? It's not like I'd touch his dick. It's more about the taboo of it." Damon kind of preferred to watch threesome porn with two guys.

"Right."

They were quiet, and then Damon yawned, shutting his eyes. "You know…we're the same height."

"So?"

"So we could have a threesome."

Elliot didn't respond, so Damon opened one of his eyes. "Cause the angles would be right," he added.

"Yeah. I got that." Elliot was staring at the ceiling.

"What's wrong?"

"Nothing."

Damon grinned. "You're thinking about it, right? It'd be hot as fuck. Who'd we share?"

Elliot groaned dramatically. "You have a girlfriend. Should we really be talking about this?"

"Oh, come on," Damon said. "It's just a fantasy. Do you want to share Rochelle with me?"

"Dude! Rochelle would not appreciate you saying you'd share her with me."

Damon shrugged. "Maybe. Maybe not. She's kinda freaky. I bet she'd be into it."

"I'm not having a threesome with you."

Damon huffed. "But think about it." He laid on his back, closed his eyes, and his hand wandered into his swim trunks. "I'd be kissing the back of her neck, and you'd be kissing her tits, and she'd be making noises and grabbing on to your back, leaving red marks on your shoulders—"

"What are you doing!"

"What?" Damon said, his dick getting rock hard in his hand. "I'm just thinking about how she'd bite and lick your neck, and you'd probably moan, and while you two were busy with each other, I'd lube up—"

"Damon," Elliot said, but his voice was no longer upset. It was low and needy.

"Are you touching yourself?" Damon asked, not daring to open his eyes, wanting to stay in the fantasy, wanting to make sure nothing disturbed the images in his head.

"Yeah," he said, and Damon could hear the faint noise of skin-on-skin, of Elliot's hand stroking his dick. He sensed the slight movement from just a couple inches away. "Keep going."

There was absolutely no way Damon was stopping now. "I'd lube up and fuck her ass, while you'd put your hard cock in her pussy. She'd moan and whine but wouldn't be able to move because she'd have both of us inside of her. We'd fuck her so good we'd practically feel our dicks rubbing each other inside of her."

He gasped. "Yeah?"

"Uh huh," Damon said. "I'd grab her hips and thrust up in her, and you'd have to put your hands on my chest so we could keep in rhythm."

"I'd have to touch you?" Elliot asked.

"Yeah, but her tits are rubbing on your chest, so you'd be focused on that."

"And what would you be focused on?"

Damon stroked harder and thought about it. To keep the right angle, he'd probably be looking over her shoulder, looking at Elliot's face as he fucked her. Looking at his face scrunched up in pleasure, his blue eyes soft with need.

"You," Damon said.

Elliot whimpered, and Damon felt it shivering up his spine. His balls rose up, tight, and he had to slow his hand or he was going to come, and he wasn't ready for this to be over.

"Because I'd, you know, have to keep the right pace with you."

"Uh huh," Elliot said.

"We wouldn't come inside her though," Damon said.

"Where would we come?"

"I'd keep the same rhythm with you, so we'd time it perfect to come together, and we'd pull out and stand beside each other, and she'd be on her knees, and we'd stroke our dicks together. We'd have to stand pretty close. Our hips and legs would have to be touching, but we'd come all over her face. Our come would mix together."

Elliot moaned, and at the same time, Damon came so fucking hard that it stained his swim trunks.

Stained them so bad that they had to sneak out of the hotel to buy him new ones. Damon told his mom he'd ripped the old pair.

It had never occurred to him that anything weird happened. They were fantasizing about fucking a girl.

But now, he was questioning which part he actually enjoyed more: the fantasy of fucking a girl together or lying in bed next to Elliot, the sound of his moans and whimpers, the feel of the bed rustling as Elliot jerked himself off, the experience of coming together.

Damon rubbed his eyes and made a frustrated noise in the back of his throat. He turned, ripped the swim trunks down from the shower curtain, and tossed them in the laundry bin before covering his face with his hands.

Fuck. Fuck. Fuck.

He was so fucked.

Chapter Nine

Damon was acting weird.

Elliot had been right to keep his sexuality a secret all these years. Sure, Damon wasn't homophobic or anything, but he was tiptoeing around Elliot, uncomfortable and tense.

When he caught Damon staring at him (on more than one occasion), Damon would panic and look away, embarrassed. Elliot pretended not to notice, mostly because he didn't know what else to do.

He might have assumed Damon was just coming to terms with Elliot having powers.

Except Damon never acted strange when Elliot used his magic. In fact, he'd started coming to Elliot for all his minor bumps and bruises.

My shoulder hurts from practice.

I stubbed my toe.

I got a splinter from helping my mom in the yard.

Elliot would wave a hand over his ailment, and just like that, it was gone. He hadn't needed to try or focus at all.

His magic was always eager to touch him.

Afterward Damon would jump around the room, singing and dancing as if Elliot's magic somehow gave him a boost of energy, made him even more Damon-like.

Damon wasn't weirded out by his powers at all.

He was weirded out by *Elliot*.

He made it a point to never touch him anymore, and he'd flinch if they accidentally brushed against one another. He dropped a plate that he was passing at the dining room table when their fingers bumped.

They stopped playing video games side-by-side, too. Instead, Damon sat on the bed, while Elliot was on the floor. He hadn't tickled him, ruffled his hair, or tackled him since the awkward wrestling match last week.

It was probably for the best, but Elliot missed it. He missed having an excuse to touch Damon. He missed his best friend acting *normal*.

Damon probably just needed an adjustment period. He'd eventually see that Elliot wasn't going to come on to him or try to fuck him or something.

He hoped so, at least.

In some ways, things had gotten better. Elliot had finally figured out the trick to get his magic to cooperate.

Unfortunately, the trick was having Damon in the same room with him.

He'd started bringing his best friend to his training lessons at the clinic under the guise that he wanted to show Damon his magic. It was easy to slip into the healing flow state when Damon was next to him. Something about his presence got the spark of Elliot's magic to catch. Fired him up and steadied his mind all at once.

"It's fine," Grandmama whispered when they were out of earshot. "Some people use crystals to align their energy, some use wands, or religious totems. You use a person. It's no big deal.

Once you get used to conjuring magic, you won't need him anymore."

"Right," he said.

Somehow, he didn't think that was possible.

"Okay, you boys go try these on, and we'll see which size looks best," Ms. Montré said, shooing them into the back of the suit rental store.

"How long do you think this is going to take?" Elliot asked Damon as they went into their dressing rooms. "I hate malls."

The fluorescent lights. The pushy salespeople. The stupid smiling people in the giant marketing photos hanging on the walls.

"I don't know," Damon said. "Like twenty minutes?"

Elliot took off his shirt and slipped on the collared button-up. Twenty minutes. It was just twenty minutes. Then they would go back to Damon's house and play games together, and that uncomfortable itch of wrongness he felt when he was overstimulated would dissipate.

"Wait. You're gay," Damon said. "You're supposed to like shopping and trying on clothes."

Elliot snorted. "Ha. Ha. Very funny," he deadpanned as he pulled on the dress pants.

"Sorry." Damon's voice lost its humor. "I shouldn't joke like that."

Elliot rolled his eyes. He left his dressing room and knocked on Damon's door. "Let me in."

"What?"

"Let me in your dressing room."

The handle unlatched, and Elliot slid inside. "Knock it off."

"I'm sorry," Damon said. "That joke was so inappropriate, and I don't want you to think I have a problem with you or that

I'm stereotyping. I was just ragging on you like we usually do, but I need to be more careful and less—"

"Damon!" Elliot grabbed his shoulders, shaking him. "Stop. Stop freaking out all the time. You can make gay jokes with me. You can be a dick like you usually are. Stop fucking apologizing for it. I don't want your apologies or for you to keep tiptoeing around like you're afraid if you touch me, I'm going to take that as an invitation to jump you."

"I don't think that!"

"No?"

"No!"

"Okay, then why did you quit cheating in our games?"

Damon licked his lips. Elliot forced himself not to lower his gaze to watch.

"I don't know what you're talking about. I never cheat," Damon said.

Elliot raised an eyebrow. "You'd shove me or mess up my hair when I was winning, and I'd kick you back, and if all else failed, your sadism would come out, and you'd tickle me and wrestle me to the ground."

Damon winced.

"We've done that once since I told you I was gay. And you freaked out." Elliot ran a hand through his hair to push it out of his eyes. "And I get it. You're uncomfortable, but I'm not going to try anything, and I know you're straight, okay? If you don't ever tickle me again, I will praise the lord, but I just want you to act normal. Alright?"

Damon rubbed the back of his neck. "Yeah. Sorry, man. I've been a shitty friend."

"Stop apologizing." Elliot flicked his ear.

Damon huffed a laugh and smacked his hand down. "Yeah, okay."

His smile didn't meet his eyes. His gaze was cast down, watching as Elliot tucked the tails of his collared shirt into his dress pants. Elliot buttoned them up and stared in the mirror, knocking his shoulder into Damon's.

Damon swallowed and met his gaze in the mirror. His eyes traveled down Elliot's body and up again. "You look nice."

Elliot smiled and fixed the collar. "You do too," he said with as neutral a tone as he could muster.

The button-up shirt fit Damon so well. The fabric pulled taut over his muscled chest and arms, making a sexy silhouette of his tapered waist. Elliot didn't see Damon dressed up often. The last dance they went to together was probably in the ninth grade. They'd both been gangly and awkward. Now, Elliot was still gangly and awkward, but Damon was the quintessential embodiment of the perfect prom date.

The perfect prom date for Chelsea, Elliot reminded himself.

He scurried out of Damon's dressing room and back into his own, grabbing the jacket and slipping it on.

"You know, you basically admitted you miss me tickling you," Damon said. "Which, if anything, makes you more a masochist than I am a sadist."

"No!" Elliot said. "I fucking hate it. Never ever do it again."

"I'm going to. Now that I know how much you love it."

"No! If you tickle me again, I'll..."

"What?" The door clicked as he opened it. "What will you do?"

Elliot stepped into the open space outside the dressing rooms. He couldn't think of an adequate punishment because Damon's eyes widened, and he breathed out, "Wow."

Elliot's spine tingled as Damon drank him in. He wanted to preen, wanted Damon's eyes to stay on him like that forever.

Ms. Montré came around the corner and clapped, snapping Elliot out of his fantasy.

"Oh, look at you, Elliot!" She came over and brushed the tops of his shoulders and yanked on the jacket to check the fit. "You look perfect. He looks so good, doesn't he, Damon?"

"Yeah," Damon said, his voice a little hoarse.

"Did yours not fit?" Ms. Montré asked.

Damon shook his head and handed over the jacket. "Too small."

She'd already grabbed alternate sizes and handed Damon a different jacket.

He slipped it on and stepped in front of the mirror. He spun around, checking the back before buttoning the jacket like a suave secret agent or something. He'd gotten a fresh haircut yesterday. It was buzzed in the back and the sides. His short, tight curls expertly shaped on the top.

Elliot was a slob compared to the perfection of his best friend. Why Damon was even friends with Elliot, a shy and pimply gamer nerd, he didn't know.

Elliot's tiny inconvenient crush was not only stupid but downright delusional.

"So handsome. Such beautiful boys." Ms. Montré said. "I can't believe you both are all grown up."

"Mom," Damon whined.

She waved him off. "I'll find ties to match your dates' dresses."

When Ms. Montré was out of earshot, Damon asked, "So if you were taking a guy as your prom date, what tie would you get?"

"Huh?" Elliot realized he'd still been staring at Damon and yanked his eyes away.

"If you were taking a guy, like, what color tie would you get since neither of you would have a dress to match?" Damon clarified.

Elliot shrugged. "I don't know. Something basic, I guess. Blue or red, maybe."

Ms. Montré reappeared and waved around a hot pink tie and a bright orange tie. "Found them!" She held them up to their necks, and they made disgusted faces at each other in the mirror.

"Kinda wish I was taking a guy," Damon mumbled.

Elliot huffed a laugh, trying to ignore the ache in his chest.

Me too, he thought. *Me too.*

Chapter Ten

Damon spent three weeks trying to figure out if he was gay.

He checked out every guy he came across and asked himself if he wanted to do anything sexual with them.

He didn't.

He watched gay porn, and found it a little...disturbing. His stomach felt vaguely unsettled through the whole thing.

He asked the internet and took stupid tests, stumbled upon internet forums, and it was all inconclusive...

It honestly just confused him more.

But since he had no proof he was gay, he must be straight, which meant he didn't have to avoid wrestling with Elliot anymore.

It was a huge relief. Damon missed touching him. He only realized how handsy he'd been with Elliot *after* he'd made the conscious decision to stop touching him.

Sitting shoulder-to-shoulder while they played video games. Squeezing Elliot's arm at school. Pulling Elliot into hugs and headlocks and messing up his hair.

You know, best-friend stuff.

Now things could go back to normal, just like Elliot wanted.

"Dude, stop."

"Sorry, I can't stop being awesome. I was born this way."

"No, you're cheating. You, lousy cheater!" Elliot shoved his shoulder into Damon's, and they fell into their usual pattern.

"I'm not cheating! You just suck." Damon gave over to his instincts, to the most natural thing in the world: horsing around with his best friend.

Shove. Push. Kick.

Controllers thrown.

And it began.

Damon smushed Elliot to the ground, and Elliot pushed his chest and flung him off. There was a little scrambling between the two as they both swung their arms trying to get the other into a headlock, but Elliot faked Damon out and went for his legs. They tumbled to the floor with a loud *thud*, stopping only a second when Ms. Montré yelled up to ask if they were okay.

"We're fine, Mom!"

"We're good, Ms. Montré!"

Then they were back at it, fumbling and elbowing and dodging. Somehow Damon got Elliot turned around so Elliot's back was against his chest. Damon locked his legs around Elliot's waist, and swooped his arm under Elliot's armpit to grab the back of his neck, getting him into a half nelson.

His other hand ended the match by fluttering his fingers on Elliot's sides.

"No," Elliot whined, elongating the word. "Stop. No. Tickling."

Damon just grinned and continued his—okay, admittedly a bit sadistic—tickling.

"I hate you!"

"No, you don't. You love me, and you love this." Damon put his hands under Elliot's shirt to get a better tickle going.

Elliot was laugh-crying, but still not calling for mercy. He started wiggling left and right, trying to slip out of Damon's hold, rubbing his ass on Damon's crotch and bending his head back so his short huffs of laughter hit the back of Damon's ear.

Elliot was so pretty with his face flushed and his eyes glistening with tears from laughter. His warm, lanky body pressed against Damon, rubbing on him.

Damon tensed, his hands stopping a second before Elliot caught up to what was happening.

They both froze.

Damon's arms loosened their hold. Elliot could have scrambled away, but he didn't.

They stayed where they were. Damon's legs wrapped around Elliot's waist, and his hardening cock pressed into Elliot's back.

Elliot was panting, his chest moving in rapid pulses. "Damon?"

"Yeah," he croaked. His throat was tight. The room seemed hotter.

"It's fine. It doesn't mean anything."

Damon's face heated, and his palms began sweating.

"It happens, man," Elliot said, trying to be nonchalant, but there was a hitch in his breath.

Damon wiped his sweaty palms on his pants, glancing over Elliot's shoulder to his lap, to the growing bulge pressing against Elliot's mesh shorts.

Something warm twisted inside of him. A slow, prideful smirk took over Damon's face. His chest puffed out a little.

Ha! Yes! Elliot *was* sexually attracted to him. He laid awake at night, annoyed that Elliot claimed Damon wasn't his type, but now he had proof that was a lie.

And…Damon had the proof that he might not be so straight after all.

He inhaled a ragged breath and blew it out slow. Elliot shivered a little.

Damon rested his hands on Elliot's thighs, near his groin. He could still play all of this off as an accident. One big accident.

But Damon didn't want that. Had any of it really been an accident? Any of it at all? From the moment he'd met him, Damon knew Elliot was special.

Damon slowly rubbed his hands up and down Elliot's thighs, brushing closer and closer to the tented area, waiting for Elliot to stop him, to get up and leave.

He didn't.

Damon's hand slid over Elliot's hard length. Elliot sucked in a breath as Damon thumbed the head through his shorts.

"Do you remember when we jerked off together at the beach?" Damon asked.

"Yeah," Elliot said, voice rough as sandpaper.

"I think about that all the time."

"Having a threesome?"

"Yes. No. Sorta." Damon's hand traveled lower, gently cupping Elliot's balls. He found he wasn't repulsed by this at all. Touching a guy's balls.

Damon was the opposite of repulsed. He wanted to explore Elliot's body. Wanted to see him.

"I think about the noises you made," Damon said, slipping his hand under Elliot's shirt. "About how fast you came. How fast I came. How it's the only thing I jerk off to anymore."

Elliot's throat worked with an audible gulp.

Damon caressed the soft hair of Elliot's happy trail, giving Elliot a chance to stop him before Damon continued lower.

"Damon," he said, low and breathy.

He closed his eyes as Elliot's voice traveled up his spine. "Just like that. At the beach. You said my name just like that."

"What are you doing?" Elliot hissed through his teeth.

Damon flattened his palm over Elliot's stomach. He ran his nose through the straight blonde hair above his ear. He smelled so good, so unlike a girl's fruity floralness. Elliot smelled like the familiar piney musk that he'd come to associate with his best friend, with both safety and excitement. "I want to make you come."

Elliot inhaled shakily.

He waited, but Elliot didn't say anything, didn't give him permission, so he added, "Can I?"

"Yeah. Yeah," Elliot said, wiggling his hips.

Damon's hand wandered under his waistband and gripped Elliot's hard cock. "Have you been hiding this from me the whole time?"

"Yes," he said.

Damon's chest felt lighter; something euphoric filled him. "How?" Damon circled his thumb on the head to spread the precome.

"I have a spell to help constrict blood flow so it's not as obvious."

"That's convenient."

Elliot's legs were trembling.

"Are you sure this is okay?" Damon asked, removing his hands and pressing his palms to Elliot's thighs.

Elliot nodded. "Yes. It's fine. It's good. Yeah."

Damon huffed a laugh, his lips near the back of Elliot's ear. He tugged on Elliot's shorts, and Elliot pushed them down to just above his knees. Damon didn't hesitate to grip him under the head and give him an exploratory stroke.

His dick was hot and smooth, and from this angle Damon could simply be jerking himself off. Except he wasn't. This was

Elliot. Elliot quivering in his arms. Elliot panting into his ear. Elliot's precome leaking onto his fingers. Elliot's hands squeezing his thighs.

Elliot's moans as Damon licked and kissed up the side of his neck. He tongued the outside of his ear, sucking and nibbling the lobe as he jerked Elliot faster.

His other hand wandered over Elliot's hip, and along his torso, for once being extremely careful to not tickle him. He brushed over his nipples, and Elliot thrust up a bit.

Hmm, so he liked that.

Damon fingered one nipple and then the other, playing with the hard buds until Elliot said, "Damon, I'm close."

"Come for me then," he whispered into his ear, eyes locked on Elliot's lap.

Elliot tensed, his fingers dug into Damon's thighs, knuckles white. He choked out an agonized moan that Damon cut off by slapping his hand over Elliot's mouth so his mom didn't hear.

Elliot's come coated both of his thighs and Damon's right hand. He slumped and leaned back, resting on Damon's chest.

Damon released his mouth, and Elliot's head lulled a little as if following his retreating hand. He reached over to grab a tissue to clean them up. Neither of them said anything as Damon wiped his hand and Elliot's legs clean.

Elliot leaned forward to pull up his shorts, but instead of returning to his position—a position Damon would have gladly spent the rest of the night in—he turned around, kneeling in between Damon's legs.

Elliot licked his lips. His hesitant gaze darted between Damon's lap and his eyes. "Do you want me to…"

Damon was so fucking hard it hurt, but he tried to play it cool. "I mean, not if you don't want to. You don't have to do me any favors."

Elliot's pretty blue eyes blinked at him in slow motion. "Do you want me to touch you? Make you come?"

Damon's heart started galloping away. He could only nod.

Elliot knee-walked to the side of Damon's legs, giving him the space to lift his hips and pull down his pants and underwear. His dick slapped his stomach as it came free.

Elliot's hand caressed his thigh, over his hip, and pushed up his shirt a little. "Do you want to lay back?"

Damon nodded again. He'd do whatever Elliot said. Anything. Anything. He just wanted his hands on him.

He laid on the carpet of his bedroom floor, and Elliot pushed up his t-shirt so his stomach was exposed to the air. Elliot lowered his mouth to Damon's abs and kissed along the ridges of his muscles.

When he kept going lower, Damon realized with a start that Elliot wasn't going to get him off with his hand. Damon lifted up on his elbows so he could watch.

Elliot's kisses traveled down the length of his cock, his lips sucking and his tongue licking and teasing.

"Elliot," Damon moaned. "I'm not going to last long here."

The corner of Elliot's mouth quirked up. He grabbed the base of Damon's cock and put it in his mouth, sucking him down.

Damon threw his head back as pleasure licked up his spine, desire pooling in his stomach as every suck of Elliot's mouth made something inside of him pulsate with need.

When he hit the back of Elliot's throat, Damon was the one moaning too loud this time. "Oh my God. That's so good. So fucking good."

Elliot hummed, and the vibration reverberated throughout Damon's body.

"You've done this before?"

He hummed again.

"With who?"

Elliot didn't answer. He licked down his hard length until he got to the base and gently sucked on his balls.

Damon's hips bucked. A growl of frustration and pleasure escaped.

"Who did you do this to, Elliot? Who? Tell me." His fingernails scraped along Elliot's scalp, and he twisted some of Elliot's hair in his grip to tug him up.

Elliot popped off of him. "Really? You want me to talk now or keep going?" He jerked Damon once to show him what he was missing.

"How many times have you done this with someone?" Damon asked, unable to keep the harsh bite out of his voice.

He shrugged. "How many times did Rochelle give you head?"

Damon's jaw dropped. "We dated for two years. I don't know. I lost count."

Elliot shrugged again. "That many times then." And his mouth went back to work.

But Damon wasn't satisfied. Something like acid joined the heat in his belly. He yanked on Elliot's hair again. "So you basically had a boyfriend!"

Elliot sat up. "I'm doing my best work here. You're distracting me."

"Tell me who."

His hand disappeared between Damon's legs, cupping his balls. Without conscious thought, Damon's legs spread.

"Benjamin Kidnak," Elliot said.

"Benjamin was your boyfriend?"

Elliot snorted. "No. I used to suck him off whenever he got bored with whatever cheerleader he was dating that week."

Damon clenched his jaw. "You're not with him now." It wasn't a question. It was a demand.

His face softened. "No. I'm not. Right now, I'm with you. Trying to give you a blowjob."

Elliot rubbed some spot under his balls, and Damon collapsed onto his back, biting his finger to hold back his moan.

I'm with you.

I'm with you.

The words played on repeat as Elliot continued to perform his magic. It must be a healing witch thing because Damon had never felt like this before.

"Elliot, I don't know what you're doing to me, but I'm going to come."

Elliot didn't pull off of him. He only hummed and sucked and stroked him harder until Damon exploded. The pleasure barreled into him faster and harder than he could comprehend. He mumbled Elliot's name over and over as his body shook.

His muscles gave up, and a little shiver ran through him as Elliot swallowed his come and licked him clean.

Damon's mouth hung open as he watched Elliot sit back on his heels and wipe his mouth on his arm. He smirked at Damon's wrecked expression.

"Holy shit. That was…" He couldn't find words.

Elliot snorted, and Damon realized he liked Elliot this way. This cocky, confident guy who could wreck him with his blowjob skills.

"What? Rochelle didn't deep throat you?" Elliot asked.

Damon laughed. "No. She didn't play with my balls either. Jesus that was…" He rubbed a hand down his face.

Life changing.

And no, not because he'd never been deep throated before.

Elliot's cheeks reddened, and Damon realized he liked Elliot this way too. The sensitive, shy guy who got embarrassed by compliments.

Shit.

Maybe Damon just liked Elliot in every way he could get him.

He pulled up his pants and sat, leaning against the bed as that truth washed over him.

They were silent. Not looking at each other. Not making a single move.

"So?" Elliot said. "Ah. We can...we can, you know, forget that happened."

Damon opened his mouth, but he didn't even know what he was going to say.

Damon's mom yelled from the kitchen, "Boys! Dinner is ready."

They looked at each other for a beat before averting their eyes.

Elliot stood and stuttered, "I'm—I'm, uh, just going to—to clean up in the bathroom."

"Okay."

Damon took a deep breath to collect himself and went downstairs.

Chapter Eleven

What. The. Fuck.

Elliot ran his hands under the faucet as if washing them would make them stop glowing. His power churned in his gut, hot and fast, like a disturbed hornet's nest. His blood was pumping with adrenaline and magic. Every part of his body was extra sensitive. Like he could hear, see, taste better. Like some freaking superhero.

He'd never felt an orgasm like that. Had never felt anything like that in his life. He wanted to run out of the house and find someone to heal. Show up at the hospital and empty out the emergency room in two point eight seconds flat.

He clenched his hands into fists, and the light finally went out, though he was still shaking.

If there was any doubt that Elliot's magic was somehow tied to Damon, it was gone now.

Don't take the bait, decrease my heart rate, he recited the spell that practically never worked.

His magic flickered, and a single wave of calm flooded him. Elliot sighed in relief. He slumped against the sink. His mind cleared enough that he could actually think.

What was that?

They'd been wrestling for years, so what had changed? Maybe it was a fluke. Stimulation would make anyone aroused. Like Elliot told Damon in the beginning, it didn't mean anything. Maybe Damon had just been curious. Maybe he'd been imagining jerking himself off and was imagining a girl giving him a blowjob.

Although, he had kept moaning Elliot's name.

And he was all bent out of shape about Benjamin. What was *that*?

Oh God.

Elliot ran his wet hands through his hair as the realization sank in.

That was him losing his best friend.

He'd thought telling Damon that he was gay had changed things between them...

This? *This*? Damon would never talk to him again.

Elliot would have to pretend nothing happened. They'd agreed to forget it. So that was what he'd do.

Forget. Forget all about sucking off his best friend. The best friend he'd had a crush on for as long as he could remember.

Yeah.

Right.

Elliot padded into the dining room where Ms. Montré and Damon were dishing out food.

"Uh, so I'm really sorry, but I just realized I need to get home," he said.

Damon's head whipped up. "Why?"

Elliot winced. Ms. Montré was watching them with curiosity. He swallowed. "My mom wants me to help her...uh, with the mulching. Yeah. She, uh, got a shipment, and it's too heavy for her to spread, and my dad hurt his back so..."

Damon glared at Elliot. "You can't leave. You can't! You were...going to help me with my math homework."

Elliot worried his lip.

"Please," Damon said, the word a broken plea. "I need you—your help, I mean."

Elliot's willpower cracked. He'd never been able to resist Damon's sad eyes. He couldn't deny him anything.

"Text your mom and tell her we'll do the mulch together next weekend. It'll get done twice as fast," Damon said.

Elliot pulled out the chair beside him and sat down at the table. "Yeah, okay," he mumbled and pretended to pull out his phone to text his mom.

Damon took a deep breath and sighed it out, passing the bowl of pasta to Elliot after taking his helping.

Their fingers touched, and they shared a look that Damon broke first.

Damon pushed his food around his plate and gave his mom one-word answers about school and baseball, forcing Elliot to make up the slack.

After dinner, all Elliot wanted to do was go home and stare at the ceiling and try to figure out what the hell was going on. He needed to be alone to think about how he should act. He didn't know the best way to go about this. Did they have a mature conversation about it? Did they continue to pretend it didn't happen? Did Elliot suck it up and admit his feelings?

Ha. No way.

Elliot was distracted by these thoughts as he followed Damon to his room, which was why he let out an embarrassing squeal when Damon grabbed a handful of his shirt, pulled him inside, and pressed him against the closed door.

"I couldn't let you leave. I can't..." Damon squeezed his eyes shut. "Please. I don't want to fight like last time."

"We're not," Elliot said. "We're not fighting."

"I can't handle you avoiding me. Us not talking," Damon said, his knuckles white as if he could hold Elliot there with him through pure strength of will.

"It's okay, Damon," Elliot said, grabbing his wrist, which loosened his hold on his shirt. "I'm not going anywhere—"

Damon launched forward, silencing his next words with a kiss.

Elliot tensed, his confusion and shock freezing him in place for a split second, and then his power lit him from the inside out, the heat from his magic and his desire melting him, making him pliable and moldable to Damon's wandering hands.

Damon's mouth slotted over Elliot's, and his stubble scraped along Elliot's cheeks, rough and biting. Damon flattened his palms over his chest, up his shoulders, grabbing either side of his jaw and forcing Elliot into whatever position Damon wanted.

Elliot finally regained some motor function and let his hands travel under Damon's shirt, reveling in the peaks and valleys of Damon's ab muscles under his hands. He'd always wanted to lick them, wanted his mouth on them. That had been the very first thing he did when Damon had let him touch him. He was obsessed with his body. Had been for so many years. And now it was pressing into him and he was free to touch it all he liked.

Elliot wound his hands to Damon's back and kneaded the lean muscles along his spine and down toward his ass. He hesitated for a second, but Damon was nipping at his bottom lip and sucking it into his mouth, so Elliot squeezed the round muscled flesh of his ass and used that leverage to pull their groins closer, practically humping him. He tried to memorize the ecstasy that was Damon's body against his. It'd been so much better than Elliot had ever let himself imagine it could be.

Damon ground his pelvis against Elliot's, their hardening dicks rubbing against each other.

Frantic need erupted; power burst from Elliot's hands, but neither of them noticed or cared. Every cell of Elliot's body was singing Damon's name in perfect harmony.

Damon's tongue was mouth fucking him, vicious and demanding, with so much need it made Elliot want to know what it'd feel like if Damon really fucked him. What it'd feel like to have more than just Damon's tongue inside him, to have all of him inside of him. Damon was already imprinted in Elliot's every cell. They grew up together. Every cherished memory Elliot had had pieces of Damon in it.

"Damon," Elliot moaned as Damon kissed and nipped his jaw, but he shouldn't have broken the silence because in the next second Damon was gone, backing up with scared wide eyes.

Elliot put his hand out, but Damon only stared at it like it was poisonous.

"Hey. It's okay. It's fine." It wasn't. But Elliot could pretend. He'd been pretending for years.

"We can't..." Damon rubbed his eyes. "I'm not..."

Elliot sighed. "You aren't gay?"

He shook his head.

Elliot pressed his lips together. "Is it possible that maybe..."

He stared at him like the next words out of his mouth might cause an explosion and destroy everything.

Hell, maybe they would.

"Is it possible that you're bisexual?" Elliot asked.

Damon stepped backward until his knees hit the bed, and he sank down. He put his head in his hands. "Yeah, I guess so."

"I can go," Elliot said. "I don't want to upset you."

"No." He looked up with tears in his eyes. "Please don't leave. I...I have no one to... I need my best friend."

Elliot's heart broke at the anguish in Damon's voice. He sat beside Damon on the bed and wrapped his arms around him. Damon buried his head into Elliot's chest and sobbed.

"It's okay," Elliot said, rubbing his back. "It's going to be okay."

"I don't want to lose you. I can't lose you."

"You won't. You'll never lose me."

The last time they were in this exact position was when Damon's dad died. His dad had been amazing, funny and jovial, just like Damon. If he was still alive, Damon could have gone to him. Could have told him what he was feeling.

But Damon didn't have his dad anymore. As much as Elliot was confused and upset and heartbroken over whatever was happening between them, it was ten times harder for Damon.

"I'm not going anywhere, Damon." Elliot held him tighter and hoped the sentiment said what he couldn't. What he'd been unable to admit to himself until now.

I love you.

Chapter Twelve

Elliot had let Damon blubber into his shirt, and then they watched a movie until Damon was too emotionally exhausted to stay up any longer. He'd gone to sleep with Elliot's leg pressed to his. Granted, he was above the covers and Damon was under them.

When Damon woke, Elliot was curled up on the futon.

He dragged his eyes away from Elliot's sleeping form and stared at the ceiling. He wasn't upset about being bi. He wasn't ashamed. He knew his mother wouldn't care. His dad, if he were alive, would have made some lighthearted joke about expanding his dating pool.

His teammates might be a little weird at first, but the locker room wasn't hostile like he'd heard horror stories about at other schools.

No, Damon wasn't upset that he was attracted to guys.

He was upset that he was attracted to his best friend.

That was the truth behind Damon's obsessive need to prove to himself that he didn't like guys. Behind his odd behavior toward Elliot. The truth he didn't want to acknowledge.

His mind and body never equated the wrestling and touching that they did as sexual, until the day they finally did.

He scrolled on his phone all morning trying to understand the process of how the brain "can change what stimuli it associates as sex-related."

He lived in—what the internet called—a heteronormative world. Basically, attraction to boys, bad; attraction to girls, good. He knew he was attracted to girls, so he unconsciously ignored the little inklings that might have told him something else.

He'd always wanted to touch Elliot. Wanted to be near him. Wanted to hear his voice. Listen to his stories. Be lulled by his peaceful presence.

Had always enjoyed their bodies tangled up together, Elliot's chest heaving with laughter, the brightness in his eyes when he smiled.

And now, Damon wanted their bodies tangled up in a different way, wanted Elliot's chest heaving for a different reason, wanted the brightness in his eyes to smolder with desire.

Desire for *him*.

Damon wanted Elliot.

And unless Damon turned these feelings off, he was going to lose his best friend.

Elliot stirred on the couch and turned on his side. "Hey."

"Hi."

"How are you?"

"Fine."

Elliot sat up and stretched, yawning. His shirt rode up, leaving a strip of his stomach exposed. A flash of heat zapped Damon in the groin, so he fixed his gaze back to the ceiling.

"You ready to do this?" Elliot asked.

"Do what?"

Elliot threw a pillow at his head. "Prom."

Damon caught the pillow and tossed it back at him. "Yeah. I'm ready to see you make a fool of yourself trying to dance."

He laughed. "Okay yeah. Cause you're such a great dancer."

"I am," Damon said, smiling.

He rolled his eyes. "Sure, okay. I need to run home to grab some stuff."

"Like what? Your suit is here." Panic flooded his veins. Elliot couldn't leave. If he left, he'd think about what happened. He'd avoid Damon. He'd tell him that they needed to end their friendship because he was too weirded out now.

He could not leave.

Elliot shifted. "I don't know. Underwear and shit? I didn't think I was going to stay over. Didn't really pack."

"You can wear mine." Damon got out of bed and grabbed some from the dresser and tossed them at him.

"Okay," he said with a confused uptick at the end of the word. "Guess I'll go shower then."

Damon didn't dare turn around for fear he'd see the extent of Damon's obsession with him on his face.

Elliot left. The bedroom door clicked closed. He exhaled.

The shower hissed on from down the hall.

The image of Elliot undressing, Elliot wet in the shower, Elliot wearing Damon's underwear distracted him for the next ten minutes.

He laid down, put his hands under his waistband, and tried to jerk the images out of his mind.

He was pretty sure it made everything worse.

Chapter Thirteen

Elliot's phone rang while he was in the shower, interrupting the mental spiral he was in the middle of. He wasn't quick enough to grab it before it went to voicemail. He cut his shower short and toweled off. Most people knew better than to call him, so it must be important.

His damp hands fumbled to play the voicemail on the touchscreen until finally he heard his grandmama's recorded voice.

"Hi, Elliot," she said. Her voice was strained. "Can you come over this morning? I'm not feeling well."

The wet phone almost slipped out of his hands as he scrambled to pull on Damon's underwear and his shorts. He sprinted into the bedroom, shirtless, hair still dripping. "I have to go." Bobbing around the room, he searched for his car keys. He was usually more organized than this.

"What's wrong?" Damon asked. Elliot didn't have time to revel in the way Damon's eyes lingered on his half-naked body.

"Grandmama called." Elliot yanked on one of Damon's t-shirts as he continued, "She's not feeling well."

Damon's eyes widened. He swiped Elliot's keys off his desk and handed them to him. "*She* said she wasn't feeling well?"

Elliot ran a hand through his wet hair. It'd look like crap if it dried pressed to his headrest in the car, but he didn't care. Grandmama was never sick. Never.

If she was calling Elliot for help, something was really wrong.

"I'll come with you," Damon said. His phone rang as Elliot started to protest.

Damon pressed the phone between his cheek and shoulder, answering as he pulled on socks.

"Hello?" He froze, second sock midway in the air. "Yeah, Chels. I didn't forget about picking up the flowers." Damon scrunched up his face. "Of course, I didn't forget that the flower shop closes at noon. In fact, I was getting ready to go get them now."

Elliot huffed a laugh as Damon ran a hand down his face. He hung up with Chelsea and turned to Elliot. "I'll pick up your flowers too. Text me if you need anything? If you need me to come over or—"

Elliot swallowed hard. "It's fine. I'm sure it's fine."

He wasn't convincing himself or Damon, but Elliot forced a smile, and they both raced out of the house, driving in opposite directions.

Elliot practiced the deep breathing exercises Grandmama taught him to help center his mind, but he kept coming back to the same question. What had happened that Grandmama couldn't heal herself?

The twenty-minute car ride felt interminable. As soon as he pulled up to the house, he dashed out of the car and didn't bother knocking.

"Grandmama? I'm here," he shouted as he slipped his shoes off in the entry.

She didn't answer back. Elliot's heart started pounding, the *thump-thump* heavy in his ears.

The prickle of his magic itched under his skin, adrenaline and fear igniting his nervous system responses. His core warmed, and tingles cascaded down his arms, energy trying to escape.

"Grandmama?" he called again as he went down the hall to her bedroom. He knocked on the door once before pushing it open.

She was sitting on the bed, wincing. "Can you open this?" Her hands shook as Elliot reached for the aspirin.

She looked okay enough. Was dressed and sitting up. Slightly pale, but the lighting in the bedroom was dark.

"What's wrong?" he asked, undoing the safety features on the cap and giving the medicine back.

She shook her head, grabbing the bottle, but her fingers slipped and sent little pills flying everywhere.

Grandmama gasped and clutched her chest.

"What's happening?" Elliot demanded.

"Heart," she croaked.

"I'm calling an ambulance."

"No. Don't," she gritted out. "Magic."

She wanted him to use his magic?

"I can't," he said. "You know I can't. Damon isn't here. I'll call an ambulance. I'll—"

"No. Magic is doing this. No hospital."

The little white pills on the ground. Aspirin. Wasn't aspirin for a heart attack? She'd overworked her powers. A build-up of congealed magic was clotting her veins.

He couldn't call a hospital. There was nothing they could do for a magical heart attack.

The only way to dissolve the clots was with Elliot's powers.

Nausea curled sour and thick in his stomach, but he helped Grandmama to lie down on the bed. She grabbed his wrists, tried to open her mouth to say something, but instead squeezed her eyes shut and whimpered.

The sound hit Elliot in the gut. His grandmama was never hurt, never in pain. She was invincible. She was a superhero.

Except, she wasn't. She was human.

And she was dying.

Elliot forced himself to ignore the panic locking up his muscles and closed his eyes, hovering his hands over her chest. He took a few centering breaths and tried to focus on moving the energetic prickles from his core, through his arms, to his hands, and into Grandmama's heart.

His palms tingled, but the magic swirling through him wouldn't get the hell out.

"Please, please," he murmured under his breath, mind whirling as he tried to think up a spell.

Clear her blood, remove the mud.

Nothing happened.

Strengthen my focus, clear Grandmama of this toxic hocus pocus.

Stupid. Stupid. He was stupid. He couldn't get his stupid magic to cooperate.

His powers ricocheted violently inside his body, an angry storm of high winds and pelting rain and rumbling thunder. The chaotic levels of his magic raged, threatening to send him into a panic attack unless he released the energy.

His heart rate was too high. He needed to be calm, clear.

He mumbled his heart rate decreasing spell to no avail.

He tried to bring Damon to mind. Tried to feel into the peace and safety and...love he felt when he was with him. Of desire and need.

Tears fell down his face.

He couldn't do it.

With clumsy haste, he pulled out his cell phone, calling Damon.

He picked up on the first ring. "I'm already on my way. What's wrong?"

Elliot inhaled a ragged breath. He didn't know how Damon knew he needed him. It could have simply been Damon knew his grandmama was never sick, or it could be that even though he wasn't a witch, he could tap into whatever weird connection they had too.

"I need you," Elliot said, crying into the phone. "She's having a heart attack. A magical one. I can't go to the hospital. I have to use my magic, but I can't. I need you. My magic doesn't work without you."

"Okay. Okay," Damon said. The *click-clack* of the turn signal echoed through the phone, increasing Elliot's frantic heart. "I'm on my way, but it's going to be at least twenty minutes."

"It'll be too late."

Grandmama's breathing was already shallow.

"Damon," Elliot pleaded. "She's dying. I can't—" He couldn't inhale. His chest ached. "I'm not good enough to—" His magic burned, a wild thrashing inside of him, making him shake.

"Elliot, listen to me," Damon said. "Listen. Are you listening? Take a deep breath with me, okay? Ready?" He sucked in a breath and blew it out slow. Elliot followed his cues. "Put me on speakerphone. We're going to do this together. You're going to do this."

"I can't."

"You can, Elliot," Damon said, his voice strong and sure. "You're going to do this. You don't need me. I know you can do this."

Elliot took another breath and put the phone down. His hands trembled. The magic ripped at his bones, tore through his tensed muscles, desperate to get out.

"You don't need me for your magic to work, Elliot. You just think you do. I watched you heal all those animals. I watched the magic fill you. It wanted to work for you. It wanted to listen to you."

Elliot held his hands in front of his torso, palms facing each other. He imagined the magic listening to him like Damon said. That the energy was working for him.

"You were beautiful," Damon continued. "Every single time you healed me. It was like watching the sun rise inside of you. I've never seen you so full of life as you are when you're healing, Elliot. I might have been extra careless lately just because I wanted an excuse for you to heal me. Your magic inside me makes me feel like I can fly. Like there's nothing so right in the entire world."

Elliot breathed in Damon's words, pictured himself the way Damon saw him. The magic rising and cresting. His palms lit up, white light bouncing between them.

"It's working, Damon," he said. He took his time, focusing the magic over Grandmama's heart, using his energy to strain her blood, to massage out the clumps of gloopy magic.

"Of course it is. You're amazing. I knew you could do it."

"Don't hang up," Elliot said.

"I won't," Damon said. "I promise."

Time passed in funny intervals. Elliot slipped into a flow state as his magic generated and released in easy bursts. He used the techniques his grandmama taught him to direct the magic into doing exactly what he needed.

He felt Damon arrive before he heard the front door open. He didn't call out to him. He knew Damon sensed exactly where he was.

Damon stood behind him, and Elliot sighed out a huge breath as he put his arms down. His body swayed, almost unconsciously magnetized toward Damon, wanting to be fully in his orbit.

Grandmama stirred. Her eyes opened. Elliot grabbed her hand, and she squeezed back. His magic sensed her pulse, felt the aliveness of her aura. The health of her powers.

Relieved tears sprang to his eyes.

"I knew you could do it," Damon said. He put his hand on Elliot's arm and pressed his chest into Elliot's back.

Elliot turned, and not letting go of his grandmama's hand, he buried his head into Damon's neck and hugged him.

Damon rubbed his back, murmuring soft nothings until he settled.

Chapter Fourteen

Damon knew it was wrong. He knew it was toxic. But he'd overheard Grandmama tell Elliot it was okay that his magic only worked when Damon was around.

It'd been wrong to feel something like pleasure flip-flopping in his stomach. Elliot was upset about it. He thought he wasn't a good witch. He'd blamed himself for Damon's dad's death.

But Damon liked that Elliot needed him.

It was wrong. Very wrong.

And Damon knew that Elliot's magic didn't actually need him. He was glad that was true, else Grandmama would be dead right now.

Still, that evil little voice in his head taunted him, now that things were weird between them, if Elliot's magic didn't need him, why would he keep him around?

Chapter Fifteen

Elliot and Damon tried to convince Grandmama that they could skip prom and stay with her, but she refused.

"I want you both to go," she said, smiling. "I'm fine now. Go have fun. You only have one senior prom."

They relented when Elliot's parents came over and promised to watch over her for the rest of the day.

She got a scolding from Elliot's dad for overworking herself at the clinic yesterday, but almost dying must have scared her as well because despite her dismissive attitude toward their fussing, she agreed to cut back her hours at the clinic now that Elliot was able to command his powers at will.

Which was how Elliot found himself standing in a park, trying not to sweat in his suit, as he watched Chelsea position Damon in front of one of the blooming flower trees.

Damon started making robot mouth sounds, acting like he was just a prop for Chelsea to move around as she pleased.

Chelsea playfully smacked his arm, laughing along with him. She fixed his tie and smoothed his jacket, then snuggled her body against his to pose for the cameras.

A hollow feeling permeated through Elliot. He was having a hard time getting into the prom mood.

He wouldn't have been here if he wasn't sure that Grandmama was okay, and if he were being honest, it wasn't worries about her health that was leaving him feeling unmoored.

"Hey." Madison walked up.

"Hey," he said. "Are we getting more photos?"

"I think we've taken enough, don't you?"

Elliot snorted. "Yeah, but I don't think Chelsea would agree." Madison and Elliot watched as Chelsea and Damon repositioned for another round of photos on the bridge.

Damon's smile was huge, all bright-white teeth, happiness radiating from him. He could even pull off the ridiculous orange tie. The color brought out the depths of his warm brown eyes. Chelsea looked beautiful too. They looked good together. Like a real couple.

The hollow feeling thickened and turned darker. Would prom be the beginning of their official relationship? He knew that they'd messed around a few times, but he wasn't sure how serious they were.

He didn't want to know...except he *did* want to know.

"I know I made you put on that whole scene in school, but I'm not actually all that interested in being looked at," Madison said.

"Then why did we do that?"

She sighed. "I wanted Jason back. I miss him all the time. Chelsea came up with that plan and said it'd make him realize what he was missing, but he hasn't even looked in my direction."

"I'm sorry, Madison."

She gave Elliot a sad smile. "It's fine. I don't mean to be a downer. It's prom."

He nudged her shoulder with his. "I'm not exactly bursting with joy today either."

"I noticed. Something going on between you and Damon?"

"What?" he screeched a little too loud. "No, of course not. What makes you say that?"

She kept her eyes glued on the couple on the bridge. Damon was kissing Chelsea's cheek.

Elliot had to look away.

"I don't know. He's just been watching you even more than usual, and it's almost like you're avoiding him or something." She shrugged. "I could be wrong. Maybe I'm projecting my own tragic love story."

He scoffed. "There's no tragic love story. I don't know what you're talking about."

He narrowed his eyes, thinking, and turned toward her. "What do you mean more than usual? What is usual?"

Madison shook her head, laughing. "You two are attached at the hip. Always have been. Damon is extremely protective over you. You really haven't noticed?"

"No..."

But that was the second time someone had said that to him.

Chelsea yelled Damon's name and snapped her fingers to get his attention, but his eyes were scanning the horizon until they landed on Elliot. Damon grinned.

Only a moment passed, and then he was putting his arm around Chelsea's waist and pulling her close again.

"See?" Madison said.

They were best friends. And Damon knew Elliot was all off-kilter from healing Grandmama. He was checking up on him.

That's all that was.

"Madison," Elliot said. "Can I tell you something?"

"Sure."

He straightened his spine, dipped his chin, and looked her in the eye. "I'm gay."

A soft smile spread across her face. "Thank you for telling me."

She opened her arms for a hug, and he accepted it, careful not to mess up her hair. They hugged for longer than normal. And it felt good. Really fucking good to have someone to tell. Someone he could tell without being afraid that it would change their relationship.

The hug ended, and she asked, "Is it a secret or are you officially coming out?"

He shrugged. "I don't know. I don't think I want to send out a school-wide email or anything, but I don't think I'm going to hide it anymore either."

"Okay," she said.

They were quiet for a moment, watching as Chelsea and Damon made their way toward them.

"You know, you could just tell Chelsea, then you wouldn't have to send out a school-wide email," Madison said.

Elliot laughed so hard that tears leaked from the corners of his eyes.

Damon was smiling as he came up to them. "What's so funny?"

"Your face," Elliot said. "We were discussing how much of a loser you are."

Damon stuck out his tongue. "Then you're a loser by association!"

"You're right," he said. "I need to stop hanging out with you. Your uncoolness is ruining my street cred."

Damon made the growling noise he usually did before he pounced and started tickling him, but what he did next was almost worse.

He wrapped his arms around Elliot, enveloping him, and Damon rubbed his chest against Elliot's body as if trying to wipe his essence on him.

"Ugh! Stop! You're getting all of Chelsea's perfume on me," Elliot said, laughing and pushing him away.

"If I have to smell like I bathed in flower juice, then so do you!"

Damon grabbed Elliot's face and licked his cheek. "There. You're covered in my *uncoolness*. I'm the only one that you can hang out with now." He stepped back, all smug.

"You're disgusting!" Elliot said, wiping at his cheek, as if he hadn't had Damon's saliva in his mouth yesterday…or his come.

Madison met Elliot's gaze over Damon's shoulder, her arms crossed, and an eyebrow raised as if to say, *See? Possessive.*

Chapter Sixteen

Prom was boring as fuck.

Imagine Damon's surprise when, after spending hours in a park taking pictures, the first thing he had to do when they arrived at prom was…take more pictures.

Madison pulled Elliot down the hall, while Chelsea ushered him toward the photographer set up in the corner of the gymnasium.

"More?" he groaned. "Didn't we get enough?"

"Shh," Chelsea said. "Those were outside photos. These are the official prom photos. No more after these. I promise."

"Fine," Damon said.

"Maybe just a few candids," Chelsea mumbled. She ignored Damon's long whine.

After more photos, they were both taken in different directions by friends and teammates. Damon scanned for Elliot, and uneasiness crawled under his skin when he couldn't find him.

No one was dancing. Everyone was scattered in groups, talking to each other.

Madison and Elliot reappeared, walking inside from the hall, and Damon inhaled deeply as if he'd been suffocating until he set eyes on him again.

Damon crossed the gymnasium, tuning in to their conversation before he reached the corner they'd settled in.

"You want something to drink?" Elliot asked Madison, his tone as bored as Damon felt.

"Not really."

"So this is prom?"

She laughed. "Yeah."

"To think I could be playing video games in my underwear right now."

She shoved him a little. "Huh, so you guys take your clothes off to play video games? Interesting."

Elliot was blushing when Damon grabbed his arm and saddled up beside him.

"Who's taking their clothes off?" Damon asked.

"No one!" Elliot said. His blue eyes were almost bluer when his pale skin was turning red. Even the tips of his ears were tinged pink. He was so cute when he was embarrassed.

Fuck me.

Madison giggled.

"Damnit," Damon said. "I'd do just about anything to get out of this suit." He grabbed his collar and yanked a little to loosen his tie.

Elliot swallowed, not meeting his gaze.

"You wanna?" Damon asked, patting his chest pocket.

"What?" Elliot screeched, his eyes darting to Madison and back to Damon.

"I heard you asking about a drink. I have…" he trailed off and patted his chest pocket again where he'd hidden the flask, widening his eyes to make himself clear.

"Oh. *Oh*," Elliot said. "I thought—" He shook his head and did a cute little hair flip. "Never mind. Yeah, uh, let's go."

"You go first," Damon said. "So no one sees us go in together."

Elliot walked toward the bathroom. Damon watched him the entire way. He hadn't had much of a chance to look at his best friend until now. Even from behind, walking away, he looked really good. He'd ditched the suit jacket so his button-up shirt was showing off his lean body. His blonde hair, usually stick-straight, had a little curl to it around the collar. As Elliot put his hands in both of his pants pockets, Damon's gaze was drawn to the way the fabric pulled tight across his ass. Heat gathered in his groin.

Madison laughed, and Damon startled, having forgotten she was standing there.

"You're obsessed, you know that?"

Damon worried his lip. "It's not like super obvious, right?"

"Nope. Not at all," she said with a mischievous twinkle in her eyes.

Chapter Seventeen

"In here," Elliot whispered from inside the bathroom stall when he heard the door open.

Damon snuck into the stall and huddled up to Elliot. He unbuttoned his suit jacket, pulled the flask out of his chest pocket, undid the cap, and handed it over.

Elliot blushed again, thinking about how he'd thought Damon had meant he wanted Elliot to help get him out of his suit.

Which Elliot would have gladly done.

He cringed, taking two terrible swallows of vodka before handing the flask back over, wishing the burn of the alcohol would burn the image of getting Damon naked from his mind.

Damon bounced on his feet, chugged the vodka, and gagged.

"Shh!" Elliot said, laughing at his disgusted face.

"It's terrible."

"You keep making noises and someone will catch us."

"We're fine." He took another swig before tucking the flask away. "Achek. This better do the job."

"One can hope."

"One can hope," Damon mocked in a stupid voice. "Who says that?"

"Shut up." Elliot shoved him, and Damon grabbed a handful of his shirt, pulling him in close to ruffle his hair. Except, it didn't feel like the normal chaotic messing around. Damon's hand lingered at the back of his head, almost like a caress. Elliot could have sworn Damon's eyes went to his lips for a split second, but as Damon's touch disappeared, he realized he was just seeing things that weren't there.

"Are you and Madison going to dance?" Damon asked, releasing his grip on Elliot's shirt.

"Only if she drags me out there. And only a slow dance."

"Same." He pulled the flask back out and jiggled it. "One more for the road?"

"Yeah." Elliot drank a little more and watched as Damon did the same.

"You leave first," Damon said.

Elliot slipped out of the stall, just as Benjamin walked in.

Elliot froze.

Benjamin's brows furrowed. His gaze went from Elliot to the obviously occupied stall he'd walked out of.

"Whatcha doing, Elliot?" Benjamin's grin was a little too wide.

"Nothing," he squeaked. His pulse raced, pushing magic through his veins and making him lightheaded.

Elliot knew exactly what Benjamin was thinking.

He was thinking that Elliot's red face and messy hair and disheveled shirt looked a lot like how he did after he gave Benjamin head in the backseat of his car.

Elliot smoothed down his hair as Damon opened the stall door.

His eyes narrowed slightly, and then he sighed and rolled his eyes. "Well, come on, Kidnak!" he said. "I'll let you have some to keep your mouth shut, but hurry up before I have to share the flask with the rest of the senior class."

Benjamin blinked, and his face cleared. "*Oh*. Sure. Yeah. Okay." He went into the stall.

Damon waved a dismissive hand at Elliot. "I'll be out in a second."

Elliot nodded and swung open the door, about to walk out, when Benjamin said, "You know, honestly Montré, I thought maybe Elliot was sucking you off in here." His cruel laugh echoed through the room.

Elliot's hand slipped from the handle. The door clapped shut.

"What?" Damon's voice was deadly quiet.

Elliot held his breath. He couldn't get his legs to move.

There was the sound of gulping and a shivering disgusted noise. "It's no big deal," Benjamin said. "I always assumed something weird was going on between you two."

Maybe Benjamin was already drunk.

"Why would you care? Do you like Elliot?" Damon asked.

Benjamin huffed a breath. "I like his mouth on my dick if that's what you mean."

Shoes scuffled across the tiled floor, and the stall rattled as if a body had been pushed against it.

"Listen, here, *Ben*. You're not going to touch Elliot again. You won't even look at him. If I see you come near him, I'll fucking knock your lights out. Understand?"

"Jesus! Calm down, man. I hear you! He's all yours."

Elliot's hands were shaking, but he found the wherewithal to open the door again. He strode back into the gym and walked toward the punch bowl to get a drink.

His throat was dry because he'd taken several shots of cheap vodka and not for any other reason. Not because Damon was being all possessive over him.

He's my best friend, and Benjamin was being a dick. He was just standing up for me.

Small hands wrapped around his arm. "Come dance!" Madison said.

He started to refuse, but the song slowed down, and she gave him a little pout. "Please?"

The bathroom door opened, and Benjamin staggered out. Damon was nowhere to be seen.

"Yeah, okay."

Madison pulled him onto the dance floor, and they swayed together with his hands on her waist and hers around his neck.

Elliot forced himself to wait until the second chorus of the song before he searched for Damon.

He was wrapped up in Chelsea's arms, staring down at her with a smile. She must have said something to make him laugh because his chest was shaking.

Madison followed his gaze. "Do you want to dance with him?"

"What? No. No. I'm dancing with you."

She shrugged. "Okay."

There was one more slow song before Madison was back dancing with Chelsea and the other girls. Elliot disentangled himself from the group, and Damon grabbed his arm as he was walking away. "Wanna play mini golf?"

"Yeah," he said, relieved to have a good excuse to get off the dance floor.

The cafeteria beside the gym was set up with games. It was mostly full of guys who weren't being forced by their dates to dance.

"Winner gets to finish the flask?" Damon said as they each grabbed a putter and balls.

Elliot wrinkled his nose. "I forfeit."

Damon laughed. "Okay. Loser has to finish the flask."

He grinned. "You're on."

While Damon set up at the first hole, Elliot asked as casually as possible, "So what did Benjamin say? It seemed like you guys were in there a long time."

Yes, he was being shady.

No, he didn't care.

Damon's ball didn't make it all the way to the hole. He shrugged. "Not much. He drank some of the vodka, but he won't rat us out or anything." Damon winked at him. "Your flawless school record is still intact."

Elliot ducked his head to hide his blush and focused on setting up his swing. His ball sailed past Damon's but didn't go in.

As Damon set up his next swing, Elliot nonchalantly looked around the room. "So he didn't say anything about me? I thought I heard him say my name as I left?"

Damon missed his ball entirely. His putter didn't even make contact.

"What'd you hear?" he said, adjusting his grip.

Elliot let him fidget. "Nothing. Just thought I heard my name."

"Oh, well, he didn't say anything about you."

Elliot nodded. He didn't even care that Damon was lying to him. It was sweet that he was trying to protect his feelings.

They moved on to the next hole.

"Did you—Do you like him or something?" Damon asked, pressing his tongue into his upper lip.

Elliot shook his head, not bothering to play dumb. "We've messed around, but it didn't mean anything. I don't like him that way."

Damon exhaled. "Good. Yeah, he's a dick."

"Yeah."

Damon test swung his putter a few times, his intense focus on his ball. "So do you like anyone you've messed around with?"

Just you.

"Nothing, like, serious," he said. "No more serious than you and Chelsea."

"Right." Damon swung, but the ball went way off course. Elliot catalogued his every movement, hoping Damon would confirm what Elliot had suggested: that he didn't want anything serious with Chelsea.

Or correct him that he did want to get serious with Chelsea, and Elliot could squash the delusional hope blooming in his chest that what they did last night meant anything.

He didn't give Elliot any inclination of his thoughts, and Damon's teammates interrupted their game and recruited them to their skee ball tournament before Elliot could figure out how to interpret his nonanswer.

Elliot volunteered to finish the rest of their flask. He snuck it into the bathroom, alone this time. As he downed the vodka, he forced himself to stop obsessing. He was just going to enjoy the rest of prom with his best friend.

With the alcohol in his system, Elliot managed to relax around Damon's teammates. He was pretty sure he was only like fifty percent as awkward as usual.

It was a quarter till midnight when Madison and Chelsea dragged Elliot and Damon back into the gym to dance.

Elliot sucked it up because Madison had been an easy-going date and didn't expect much out of him. Even Chelsea, other than her pictures, hadn't been demanding of Damon's time. Overall, prom went well. He got to spend most of it with Damon, which was the whole point anyway.

He tried his best to keep his attention on Madison, not letting his eyes wander, but the song was only a minute in when Chelsea said, "Oh, my strap!"

She bent down and held her ankle. "My strap broke. Madison, can you help me?"

"I can help you," Damon said, bending forward.

"No, you stay here," Chelsea said. "I'll be right back. Don't let the cheerleaders encroach. This is the prime dancing spot."

Elliot scrunched up his face. Prime dancing spot?

Madison tugged Elliot to Damon and put his hand on Damon's shoulder. "You two dance together. We'll be right back."

Damon opened his mouth. A protesting noise that wasn't fully formed words escaped, but it didn't matter because Madison was helping a hopping Chelsea off the dance floor.

Elliot glanced around. The cheerleaders *were* eyeing them. So maybe there was such a thing as a prime dancing spot?

Damon sighed, and as Elliot was about to pull away—because they could hold the spot without dancing—Damon's hands scooped around Elliot's hips and pulled him in.

"Well, we can't lose their spot, right?"

"Right," Elliot said, breathless. His hands slid up Damon's arms and held the back of his neck.

They swayed together, but it was entirely different from dancing with Madison.

Elliot wasn't as awkward and mechanical anymore. His body melted under Damon's touch. They were dancing much closer to one another than either of them had with Madison or Chelsea. The space between their bodies, electric. Charged with something vibrant. Magic created between the two of them.

"This is kinda nice," Damon said; his eyes hadn't left Elliot's.

Elliot nodded, his throat too tight to speak. His brain chose that moment to remind him that Damon had said he was beautiful. That he purposefully hurt himself just to get Elliot to use his magic on him.

"It's much better than dancing with Chelsea," Damon said.

"Yeah?" he croaked.

"Yeah, she's too short. You're..." His eyes wandered over his face. "You're perfect."

You're perfect.

You're beautiful.

Elliot's heart clenched, sharp shooting pains emanating from his chest and the center of his magic in his core.

The air thickened. The gym became too stuffy. A sickening dread filled his gut.

He couldn't do this.

Couldn't sway around with his best friend as some stupid, cheesy romantic song played in the background. Couldn't look into his eyes as he told him he was perfect.

He couldn't shove down the truth anymore. It was going to bubble to the surface. It'd been building for years. This crush that had started as an inconvenience and had evolved into a full-blown crisis.

He was in love with Damon. So in love with him it hurt not to tell him. It *ached*.

"I can't do this," Elliot said.

And he ran.

Chapter Eighteen

Damon almost blurted out something un-take-back-able. Words for the feelings that were churning through him bubbled up. His fingers tightened on Elliot's waist as they spun in a slow circle. The rest of the gym faded away. It was just the two of them wrapped up in an energy sphere of their own creation.

Damon knew that Elliot could read him, could see the longing that tightened a noose around his heart. Elliot could read the words for the feelings Damon had as if written plain as day in his eyes.

Elliot's face transformed in slow motion. From something soft and unguarded to eye-widening horror and finally, terror. He *knew* what Damon had almost said, how he almost broke their friendship irreparably.

"I can't do this."

Elliot sprinted out of the gym and into the hall, leaving Damon in the middle of the dance floor and swirling in a toxic pool of unrequited feelings.

Longing turned sour by rejection.

He'd hesitated only a moment before he was running out the door after him. He didn't have a plan, didn't know what he was doing.

It'd stung when Elliot had said he didn't have serious feelings for any of the guys he'd messed around with, but Damon could wait for him to see what he'd always known. That there was something special between them.

What Damon couldn't do anymore was hide how he felt. Hide that he wanted more. He wanted whatever Elliot would give him.

If that was just friends who messed around, it would suck, but fine. Damon could be patient until Elliot realized they were meant to be together.

He'd never been one to wait and think and plan, to need to know with certainty the way something would turn out before he acted.

He was a risk taker. He followed his heart. And Elliot was usually his voice of reason.

But love didn't need a reason.

And Damon was in love with his best friend.

He ran out of the gym, and almost caught up to Elliot as he escaped out the front doors of the school, except Ms. Benson slid in front of him.

"You can't leave. A parent or guardian has to sign you out," she said. Another teacher walked toward them, blocking the doors. Damon peered over her shoulder. Elliot's form disappeared down the sidewalk and around the corner of the school.

"I'm not trying to leave. I just—" Damon threw a hand out. "Elliot is upset. Please let me go get him. I'm not like doing drugs or drinking or something. Come on."

Ms. Benson narrowed her eyes and tilted her head. "You haven't been drinking?"

Damon opened and closed his mouth. "No, ma'am."

"Cause your breath smells like you have."

Shit. Fuck. Fuck.

"I haven't," Damon said. "Please. You let Elliot out."

"Mr. Croft slipped by us," Ms. Benson said. "But I'm not worried about him since he's an excellent student. He needed some air. Maybe you should go wait for him in the gym."

Damon huffed. The other two teachers didn't look like they were going to vouch for him.

It was moments like these Damon wondered if he had lighter skin, would he be treated different? Was being deemed "less than an excellent student" just a socially acceptable way to be racist?

"Fine." He let the unfairness burn in his belly and went back into the gym.

He went to the chair that Elliot hung his jacket on and checked the pockets, and as he expected, Elliot's phone was there.

Damon slumped down in the chair and held his head. His phone dinged, but it was only a text from his mom. She was on her way to pick them up.

Damon resigned himself to waiting until she came to sign them out.

"Where's Elliot?" Chelsea asked. Her shoe must have been fixed because she was walking fine.

"We were dancing," Damon said. "But he said he couldn't do this and ran outside. When I tried to follow him, Ms. Benson stopped me, and I can't get out."

Madison and Chelsea exchanged a look.

"There's an exit from the locker rooms," Madison said.

Damon glanced toward the other end of the gym. The door to the locker rooms was only guarded by one teacher. The other teachers stood, watching over the punch bowl in the far corner.

Chelsea smiled. "Come on, Montré. I've got a plan. You wanna get your man or what?"

"He's not my—"

Both girls raised their eyebrows.

Damon licked his lips and nodded. "Yeah, okay. Yeah. Let's go get my man."

Chelsea and Madison didn't try to get their prime dance spot back. Instead, the three of them danced at the edge of the crowd, near the locker room. The girls were making a scene, doing crazy dance moves, and as the bass of the song boomed, Chelsea kicked her leg and strategically fell down with an exaggerated holler.

Madison and Damon went to their knees and hovered over her.

"Help!" Madison shouted over top of the music.

The teacher in front of the locker room door came rushing over.

"My ankle. I think I broke it!" Chelsea yelled.

A few other teachers also made their way over. Other kids huddled around her, distracted by the commotion.

Damon stood and slowly inched out of the crowd.

He walked backward until he was a few paces away, checking that all the adults were focused on the spectacle, and then darted to the door.

Damon sprinted through the locker room, sweat gathering on the back of his neck, nerves flooding his body. He was sure Ms. Benson would somehow sense his jailbreak.

He ripped open the door to the outside and sucked in a huge breath as soon as he was in the night air.

"Freedom!" he shouted, arms raised in victory.

"Damon?"

Elliot sat on the half brick wall that separated the back of the school from the parking lot. His brows pulled together in confusion.

"Elliot," Damon exclaimed. "I basically just broke out of prison for you!"

Elliot's confusion warred with amusement, and he huffed like he was about to laugh but caught himself. "Go back in. I'm fine. I just need to think."

Damon hopped up on the wall and took a seat beside him. "I can think with you."

"No. I need to be alone."

"Why?"

"Because I can't think about what I need to think about with you sitting next to me," Elliot said, refusing to look at Damon.

"Why not?"

He blew out a breath through pursed lips. "Because I'm thinking about you, idiot."

Damon's heartbeat hadn't recovered from his jailbreak and took off at a new speed. The toxic pleasure of pride swelled in his chest. Damon tilted his head to the side and put his face in front of Elliot's, forcing him to look at him. "Good thoughts, right?"

Elliot's expression twisted into his *I'm trying to be stern* face, but it was undercut by the twitch at the corner of his lips. He exhaled heavily and jumped off the wall.

"Come on, Elliot," Damon said. "Whatever you need to think about. Just think out loud. I promise I won't interrupt."

Elliot took a deep breath, and with his back to Damon, he said, "I'm gay."

Damon nodded but kept his word and said nothing.

"And that means that I like guys."

Damon's lips pursed, his eyes narrowing. Elliot was the smartest person he knew, and if these were his thoughts...they were kinda dumb.

"And that means that I want to touch guys. I want to kiss them. I want to hold them and dance with them. I want them to look at me and tell me I'm beautiful and perfect. That they love me and that they will always be there for me."

Damon chewed on his lip. It was becoming really hard not to interrupt. He didn't want to hear this. He didn't want Elliot to like *guys*. He wanted Elliot to like *him*.

"I wish I'd never told you I was gay," Elliot said. "Because you wouldn't have wrestled with me and got hard and realized you were bi."

Damon really wished Elliot would turn around.

"Because it kills me that I'm gay," Elliot continued. "And you're bi. And we're best friends, and what happened between us didn't mean anything to you—"

Damon slid off the wall. "It did," he interrupted.

Elliot threw his hands up and turned around. "Well, okay, anything more than your bi awakening or whatever. But it meant a lot more than that to me and—"

"No, Elliot. It meant something to me too." Damon walked toward him but halted an arm's length away as terror flooded his best friend's eyes again, just like on the dance floor. Damon's next words were a gentle, pleading whisper, "You mean something to me. You're my best friend."

Elliot cringed. "I know. I know."

"And I love you."

He sighed. "I know. I know you do. I just... We can't keep kissing and doing things. Dancing and touching. I'm getting confused, and I don't know how to be your friend now."

"You aren't listening," Damon said. He grabbed his shoulders and shook him, forcing him to hear, no *feel*, the truth. "I love you."

Elliot swallowed, his eyes searching back and forth between Damon's. "As a friend?"

Damon shook his head and slid a hand to the back of his neck, gripping his hair. "You're my best friend. My favorite person.

You're the only one that I want to wrestle with"—Elliot snorted—"You're the only one that I find stupid excuses to touch and make up silly plans to trick you into coming over."

"You did steal my keys, didn't you?"

Damon smiled. "I was jealous of all the time you were spending without me."

"I was studying!" Elliot laughed.

"Yeah, and I was with Chelsea, but all I was thinking about was getting rid of her so we could hang out."

Damon put his hands on either side of Elliot's jaw. "I love you. More than a friend. More than anything platonic or innocent. I want to kiss you and hold you and dance with you. When I look at you, my heart hurts with how much I love you. My dick hurts with how much I fucking want you."

Elliot's laugh was a little watery.

"You're beautiful. You're perfect," Damon said. "I will always be there for you. I love you."

Elliot took an uneven breath. "I love you too."

Damon pressed their foreheads together. "Yeah?"

He nodded, tears in his eyes. "So much. For so goddamn long you don't even know, Damon."

"You been pining for me, Croft?"

Elliot pushed his shoulder. "Fuck you, Montré."

"You'd like that, wouldn't you?"

He rolled his eyes. "Is this how you flirted with all your girls? And here I was, jealous of them."

"Shut up." And to make sure he shut up—Damon kissed him.

Chapter Nineteen

Damon *loved* him.

His hands trailed up from Elliot's waist to his neck and cupped his jaw. Their lips met, pressing sweet and soft, before desire ignited and overtook rationality. The hungry passion between them that had been ignored and denied came pouring out. Their kisses became frenzied. Damon's tongue swept into Elliot's mouth, devouring him.

The pain in his chest, the ache of his magic, sighed in relief. It bloomed into a warm effervescence that filled his body, his limbs, and transferred to Damon from his palms.

Damon groaned into Elliot's mouth, and Elliot inhaled his sounds. Their love manifested as the sweet magic that had been stoked between them their whole life. It was the completion of a circuit that had been unfinished until now. A peace, a wholeness, a rightness that Elliot couldn't get enough of. He'd never get enough of Damon.

Damon's hands were in his hair, caressing the back of his neck, making him shiver. Elliot sucked on Damon's tongue. Heat and desire and need built in his stomach, in his groin. Magic heightened every touch.

"God, that feels good," Damon said as he tilted his head back and Elliot sucked and licked down his neck. His palms were shining, a bright star in the night sky. "Your magic feels so damn good. You feel so amazing."

Damon's hands grabbed at Elliot's shirt, scrambling toward his belt—

"Wait," Elliot gasped, grabbing his wrists.

Damon's hooded eyes stared at him. "Probably not the right time, huh?"

Elliot exhaled a laugh. "No. Maybe not."

Damon laughed, and then Elliot was laughing too, a release of pent-up feelings expelling from them.

"I thought you ran because you knew how I felt," Damon said after they'd caught their breath. "That you didn't want me to ruin our friendship by telling you the truth."

"You were upset only yesterday about being bi," Elliot said. "The last thing I'd have expected would be for you to come to terms with your sexuality and find out you had feelings for me all in one day."

Damon rolled his eyes. "I wasn't freaking out about being bi. I'd already been trying to figure that out for weeks. I was freaking out because I realized I was attracted to my best friend and didn't know what to do about it."

"Oh."

"You're really not as smart as your GPA says you are," Damon teased.

Elliot pushed his shoulders. "I'm not a mind reader!"

Damon grabbed Elliot's wrist and held them over his heart. "Okay. Well, now that I know that, I'll just have to tell you what's on my mind."

"A whole lotta nothing?" Elliot said under his breath, fluttering his eyelashes innocently.

Damon tried to give him a stern glare. "I'm thinking I must be as stupid as my best friend since only an idiot would fall for someone who constantly insults him."

"That is rude," Elliot said. "Would you like me to beat this guy up?"

"Actually, yes. It'd be entertaining to watch you kick your own ass."

Elliot laughed and rested his forehead on Damon's shoulder. "What if we considered the last four years of listening to the guy that I've had a crush on detail his every sexual encounter as punishment enough?"

"Jesus, Elliot. You've liked me for four years?"

"Maybe longer," Elliot hedged.

"I'm so sorry. I wish I would have known."

"Seriously?"

"Yeah," Damon said. "We could've been fucking this whole time. Think of all the mediocre blowjobs I got because you couldn't man up and tell me how you felt."

"Oh my god. I hate you so much."

"No, you don't." Damon's arms wrapped around Elliot, stroking up and down his back.

"I don't," Elliot whispered.

The locker room door swung open, the metal hitting the brick with a loud *crunch*.

"Mr. Croft! Mr. Montré!" Ms. Benson yelled. "You're both getting detention."

Elliot's heart stuttered. The ground moved under his feet. He couldn't get detention. He never had detention. Would they revoke his college acceptance if they found out?

"Ms. Benson," Damon started. He pulled his phone out of his pocket, checking a text. "It's a quarter after midnight, which means the dance ended fifteen minutes ago. And if you check the sign-out sheet, you'll see that my mom already signed us both out, so giving us detention would not really be fair as we haven't broken any rules."

She opened and closed her mouth, and then looked at her wristwatch. "I will not be sorry to see you graduate, Mr. Montré."

Damon smiled. He grabbed the back of Elliot's neck and turned toward the parking lot. "Same, Ms. Benson."

Elliot held on to Damon's waist as they walked. "I thought we were busted for sure."

"Nah," Damon said. "I got you covered. Always."

"Were Madison and Chelsea mad that we lost their prime dancing spot?"

Damon grabbed his hand, interlacing their fingers. "You know what? I don't actually think there was a prime dancing spot. I think they were trying to set us up."

Elliot snorted. "It worked."

"Yeah. They're going to be thrilled when I push you against the lockers and make out with you on Monday."

"Please don't. I don't want to get detention."

"Fine," Damon said. "I'll save the kissing for later when I'm trying to distract you from killing my team."

"So you admit it! You do cheat!"

"Nah, I wasn't cheating." Damon picked up their interlocked hands and kissed Elliot's knuckles. "I just needed an excuse to touch you."

Epilogue

"You have forty-five minutes until your next class. You can play one round," Damon said, his brown eyes pleading.

Elliot sighed dramatically and tossed his backpack onto his bed. He launched toward the console under the TV and grabbed the only controller that Damon *hadn't* gotten gunked up with peanut butter.

"Yes!" Damon said as Elliot tossed him a sticky controller and plopped onto the beanbag.

Elliot and Damon got into the same college and had, of course, decided to room together. They practically lived together anyway.

The summer after senior year had been spent the way all of their summers were spent—video games, pool parties, and not much else—except for one little difference.

There was a lot more kissing...and other stuff.

Damon's mom walked in on them while they were hot and heavy within the first two weeks that they officially got together. She was less surprised with what she saw than either of them thought she'd be.

Elliot came out to his mom and dad, and they, too, were unsurprised that Elliot and Damon were dating.

"Just use protection," Elliot's mom had said.

Elliot's face heated, and he hid behind his hands. "Mom!"

"Of course, Ms. Croft," Damon said, grinning, completely shameless.

Their first semester of college had been harder than either of them had anticipated. Elliot had to figure out how to juggle his courses and working part-time at the vet clinic, while Damon did the same with his classes and collegiate-level fall conditioning for baseball.

Second semester was easier, or maybe they'd finally gotten into the swing of things. Breakfast, class, lunch, class, work or baseball practice, dinner, video games, getting each other off.

"Hostiles in the upper attic portion," Damon said.

"Where?"

"The floor with the hole. You have to jump off the stairs to get to it."

"What the hell are you talking about?"

Damon shoved Elliot's shoulder with his foot. "Over there!"

"Where?"

"Oh my god!" Damon walked his player into a relatively safe corridor and crawled over to Elliot. He hovered over him from behind, wrapping his arms around him and covering his hands with his own. Damon's thumbs nudged Elliot's player in the right direction.

"There," Damon said in a huffy breath that tickled his ear. Elliot's head fell to the side, giving Damon more access to his neck. "You see it now?"

"Uh huh," Elliot said, letting Damon's hands do all the work of killing the hostiles while on his controller.

"You suck at this game."

"No, I don't," he said. "You suck at life."

"Wow. Good one."

Elliot turned his head, their mouths inches away from one another.

Damon's eyes darted from the screen to Elliot, falling to his lips. "We could be quick."

"If you wanted to fool around, you should have just said so," he said.

"I was trying to get you more hours on this game so you didn't completely embarrass our team when we played as a squad tonight." Damon tossed the controller and climbed onto Elliot's lap, his knees squishing into the beanbag.

"Oh, you're embarrassed of me, huh?"

"Yep. Your skills are terrible," Damon said, cupping his jaw.

"All of my skills?" Elliot nipped at his thumb.

Damon's mouth hung open, eyes hooding as he watched Elliot's lips wrap around his thumb and suck. "Well...you know, it's always good to get practice in."

"I kinda want you to fuck me," Elliot said.

Damon's nostrils flared. "Do we have time?"

Elliot shrugged one shoulder. "Yeah, I can skip my next class."

"I don't want you to get behind, then you'll spend more time away from me."

"Ugh, Damon. Please, just—"

"We shouldn't."

"Damon," he whined.

"Sorry, Elliot! Your schooling is important to me." He moved to get off him.

Elliot hooked his fingers into his waistband. "Fine! I lied, okay?"

Damon raised an eyebrow.

"I don't have class on Monday, Wednesday, Friday at eleven, okay? I told you I did because that's when I go to the library to study."

Damon's jaw dropped. "You little liar." He squeezed his thighs on either side of Elliot so he couldn't escape and started tickling him.

"No, stop!"

"This is your punishment for lying to me," Damon said, grinning wickedly as Elliot wiggled and squirmed under him.

He tried to grab Damon's hands, but Damon flattened himself onto Elliot and wrapped his legs around his, using his body to press one of his arms into the beanbag.

"Damon, come on!" Elliot tried to catch his breath but just kept laughing. "You just said that"—giggle—"my schooling is"—giggle—"important."

His left hand was flopping around, trying and failing to free himself. Damon grabbed his wrist and pinned him.

"It is, Elliot. You didn't need to make anything up. You should know that I don't want to get in the way of your schoolwork. Not that you need to be even smarter."

"I know," he said. "I did it for me too. It helped to think of it like a class I couldn't skip. So I didn't, you know, end up on the floor with your dick rubbing against mine."

Damon ground down on top of him. "Like this?"

"Yeah," he moaned.

"Do you want to go study?"

"No, I want you to fuck me."

Damon didn't ask again. He pressed his mouth to Elliot's. Their tongues met, hot and eager, erasing any lingering doubts about what they should be doing with this time. Elliot gave over the heat of his magic, of his need for Damon. It was always like this. Always this intense. He fell into the all-consuming fire of his desire.

He ran his hands up Damon's neck, brushing his fingers along the soft buzzed hair at the back of his head.

Damon kissed his jaw and down his throat, then licked a slow line up his neck, dragging his tongue from his collarbone up to the curve of his ear.

Elliot's eyes fluttered shut. His fingers clenched and released on Damon's shoulders. They both pulled back to shuck off their shirts, and Damon went back to working him up into a frenzy.

He kissed and nipped and sucked on his nipples, leaving Elliot moaning and writhing and repeating his name over and over.

Damon kissed him long and deep enough that Elliot's palms started lighting up with magic. Damon grinned into the kiss, pulling back to smirk at him. "I love that your magic tells me when you're super horny."

Elliot gave him a bland look, and thrust his hips up under Damon. "Cause my boner isn't enough?"

"Oh, your boner is more than enough," Damon said, eyebrows waggling. "But I know you can hide a boner from me. Your magic, though? It's been obsessed with me lately."

It had been. Once Elliot and Damon got together, his magic spiraled through him at new levels.

Grandmama's theory was that his magic had been blocked. That keeping his crush on Damon a secret had been impeding Elliot's energetic flow.

"I don't blame it," Damon said. He ran a hand over his own naked chest, across his toned pecs and down the ridges of his abdominals, like a striptease. "I am pretty fucking amazing. I'd be obsessed with me too."

Elliot pushed Damon—an excuse to squeeze and knead those beautiful muscles—and toppled them both off the beanbag. "Can you shut up and fuck me already? Or do you wanna stare at yourself in a mirror instead? I can just go—"

"Hey, remember when you said I was three levels hotter than you?" Damon said. "I miss the days when you complimented me."

Elliot rolled his eyes. He grabbed the back of his boyfriend's head and kissed him. Elliot's hand skated down Damon's body and rubbed his erection over the top of his jeans. "You're so fucking hot, Damon. I want your big cock inside of me. I want you to fuck me until I can't remember my own name." He undid the button on his jeans and pulled down the zipper, sneaking his hand into Damon's boxers. He stroked his dick as best as he could at that angle. "How was that for a compliment?"

Damon inhaled raggedly. "I know you're patronizing me, but that was still really hot."

Elliot chuckled, and they both got rid of the rest of their clothes in a hurried, messy jumble of limbs. They were still on the floor. Neither had enough of the logical portions of their brains turned on in that moment to move to the bed.

Damon straddled Elliot and reached up to the nightstand drawer to grab the lube and a condom before he was back again, chest to chest, lips to lips. He kissed Elliot and teased his cock with slow, torturous strokes.

Elliot thrust up into his hand impatiently.

Damon smirked, not increasing his pace, letting Elliot dangle at the edge of *not enough* and *just a little more*.

Elliot's fingernails dug into Damon's shoulders. "Please, Damon."

The bastard removed his hand.

"Ugh!" Elliot was about ready to wrestle Damon to the ground and take what he wanted, but Damon leaned forward and got a little more lube, coating his fingers to tease the outer rim of Elliot's hole.

Elliot settled down.

"This what you want?" Damon taunted.

"Uh huh," he whined. "Yeah. Yeah. Yeah."

He wiggled his hips until Damon's finger breached his hole, and he moaned at how good it felt when Damon was inside of him.

Damon craved Elliot's pleasure. He shook in anticipation of how Elliot's eyes would go blank and unseeing, fucked up from what Damon could do to him. He fingered his hole, slow and teasing, brushing against his prostate on every third thrust to drive Elliot crazy.

His boyfriend's face was flushed, and his blue eyes glistened with need. That possessive part of Damon swelled in his chest every time Elliot moaned and wiggled and sighed.

"Damon," he begged.

Damon's cock leaked precome when Elliot said his name. He slipped a third finger inside of him and spread his fingers, stretching Elliot out and rubbing his prostate with intense precision.

"God, that's good. Yeah."

Damon licked his lips. "You ready for me?"

Elliot nodded frantically.

Damon grabbed a condom and lubed up. They'd both been tested since they'd gotten together, but cleanup was easier with a condom, especially since the shower was down the hall.

Elliot watched Damon's cock with heated interest until it disappeared between his legs and notched his opening.

Damon didn't tease either of them anymore. He pushed in slow, always careful. When he was fully sheathed inside of Elliot, Damon leaned forward, hands on either side of his head, starting slow and watching for Elliot's reactions.

A dazed smile spread across Elliot's face, and his hands ran up and down his torso, rounded his hips, and grabbed Damon's ass, making him move faster, harder, rougher. His magic warmed his palms and sank inside Damon, making him see stars.

"Elliot," he moaned, reveling in the feeling of being this close to him. He'd always wanted this closeness. Closer and closer and closer. He'd never have been satisfied with just sitting together or wrestling or touching. He'd always wanted more but never knew what it was that he needed until he finally had it.

Elliot's magic twisted through him like it was branding the insides of his veins. Tying them together. The heat settled in his dick, tightened his balls, made every pleasure they experienced together better.

Elliot pulled Damon down for a kiss. Their tongues intertwined, and their bodies pressed together as Damon picked up the rhythm and angled his hips until he hit the place that made Elliot gasp into his mouth.

Damon wasn't going to last much longer, not with Elliot's sounds and the way his tight hole was clenching around him. He reached down and stroked Elliot's cock.

"Uh, uh, uh," Elliot said, eyes hooded, mouth parted. He was so beautiful.

"Do the thing," Damon said, breathless.

"How bad do you want it?" Elliot taunted.

It was payback, Damon knew. For how Damon had teased Elliot earlier. He screwed his eyes shut, his body shivering in anticipation. Elliot forcing him to beg only made the whole thing even hotter.

"So bad. Please, Elliot," he said, low and tortured. "I need it. I need you. Please do it."

Elliot's hands ran up Damon's thighs, and he mumbled the spell into Damon's ear, "Sacred magic flow from me, give my lover pleasure times three."

Damon grunted, his body tightening, trembling. The ghost of an orgasm floated through him. A wave of pleasure that just kept coming and coming. Elliot's magic did something inside of him. Stimulated his prostate or massaged the pleasure centers in his brain. He tried to pay attention to Elliot explaining it one day, but he was too distracted by how good it felt to remember the specifics.

"Fuck yeah," Elliot said. "So good, Damon. Look at you."

Damon couldn't help it—he whimpered. His thrusts were uneven. The white-hot electricity of Elliot's magic pulsed through him.

"Gonna come," Elliot choked out.

Damon's eyes snapped open to watch. Elliot's face scrunched up in pleasure. Damon stroked him harder until his come jetted onto his stomach. His release trickled over his fist.

Elliot's body clenched around Damon's cock, inducing Damon's release. The force of his orgasm practically blacked him out. His muscles gave out, becoming loose and jelly-like as he collapsed on top of Elliot, burying his head into Elliot's neck and sobbing out his moan as his hips continued thrusting in short, staccato pulses until the waves of pleasure slowly subsided.

Neither moved at first, not caring about the mess that was on both of their bellies.

Bang. Bang. Bang.

They both jumped at the sound and looked at the TV.

Game Over hovered over the screen's red haze of the game they were playing.

"It's honestly surprising we didn't get killed sooner," Elliot said.

"Maybe they were enjoying the show. Your loud-ass moaning probably carried over the headset."

Elliot flicked Damon's ear. "I do not moan loudly. *You* moan loudly."

Damon pushed up and kissed Elliot's nose. "Yeah, I guess I do. Our sex is just that good. We should film a porno. I bet we'd get famous."

"Oh, yeah? You wanna share me with the world?"

Damon's face fell. "No." He wrapped his arms around Elliot's neck, his legs around his waist, and pressed their foreheads together. "You're mine."

Elliot huffed a laugh.

"I love you," Damon said.

The amusement in Elliot's eyes faded into affection. "I love you too, Damon."

THE END

Author Note

Thanks so much for reading Elliot & Damon's story. I hope you loved reading it as much as I loved writing it!

Leaving a review on Amazon is the best way to help indie authors. If you'd like to support my work, please consider leaving a review! Don't have time? No worries—even just a star rating helps immensely.

Free Novellas

Join my author release newsletter & I'll send you two exclusive free novellas. Sign up on my website at AlexandraLarson.com/freebie.

Playlist

I Fell in Love with My Best Friend – Call Me Karizma
Bleeding Love – Leona Lewis
How Soon is Now? – Charmed Theme Song
Fall For You – Secondhand Serenade

Spotify & YouTube playlist are available on my website:
AlexandraLarson.com

About the Author

Alexandra Larson is a business woman by day and romance author by night. When she's not writing or reading, she's trying to soak up the limited amount of sun the Northern Hemisphere provides.

Sign up for her author newsletter to be the first to know about new releases at AlexandraLarson.com/newsletter.